MURDER ON WHEELS

MURDER ON WHEELS

ELEVEN TALES OF CRIME ON THE MOVE

WILDSIDE PRESS

Published by Wildside Press LLC.
www.wildsidebooks.com

CONTENTS

INTRODUCTION

KAYE GEORGE

There's a story behind this anthology. The genesis was a ride my husband took a couple of years ago on the Megabus (a commercial double-decker bus that makes express runs between major cities with very limited stops). I started thinking that the bus would make a good setting for a murder: isolated setting, finite number of suspects, possible amateur sleuth. There was one problem—where to hide the body. So I asked the group, Austin Mystery Writers, for suggestions. I had been a member of AMW when I lived in Texas and we met weekly to critique each other. We're still in contact online, hence the discussion about the Megabus. Once we got started, the members of Austin Mystery Writers came up with murder scenarios on vehicles, then expanded that to include all sorts of wheels. We're all mystery novel writers and some of us have written multiple short stories. But now we all wanted to write short stories on our theme. Voila: Murder on Wheels.

We worked very hard on our projects, helping each other along the way. When we thought we needed a few more entries, we invited a couple of accomplished writers outside our group, Earl Staggs and Reavis Wortham, to contribute. We were delighted when they both said yes!

Ramona DeFelice Long was an easy choice for us as editor, since some of us had worked with her previously and found her professional, astute, and a delight to deal with.

This anthology runs the gamut from historical to present day, from Texas to Alice's Wonderland, from heavy to light. We hope you enjoy our wheelie mysteries as much as we enjoyed putting them together!

A NICE SET OF WHEELS

KATHY WALLER

When the stranger stepped through the door, everyone in the store looked up. Old men playing dominoes at the Formica-topped table beside the front window. Farmers sitting in metal lawn chairs, their boot soles propped against the cold pot-belly stove, cussing Khrushchev and the Russians. Teen-aged girls wearing shorts and white blouses, pink hairnets protecting their pin curls, looking at the makeup shelf.

They checked out the worn jeans, the frayed collar on the plaid shirt, the scuffed boots. The beat-up old black suitcase he carried. The black hair close-clipped but with a lock falling across his forehead. The scar on his cheekbone. The eyes like pale blue ice.

In those few seconds he stood in the doorway, with the sun shining through the screen door behind him, they sized him up.

He didn't look to left or right, just walked straight to the counter. I should have asked how I could help him, but I didn't. I was holding my breath.

"Are the Coca-Colas cold?"

I nodded at the cooler half hidden by a rack of chips. He opened the lid and pulled out a king-sized bottle, shook it a bit to get some of the water off, and brought it to the counter. I took it from him and dried it with a clean terry cloth towel I kept behind the counter, then gave him the towel to dry his hands. When Uncle Harry sold Cokes, he let the bottles drip. He said if customers wanted them ice cold, they'd have to put up with a little water. But I like to make things nice.

I handed him the Coke and pointed to the bottle opener nailed to the end of the counter.

"That'll be a dime," Uncle Harry shouted from behind the meat counter at the back of the store. "Seven cents if you drink it here and leave the bottle."

The man pulled a dime from his pocket and dropped it into my hand. "I'll bring the bottle back tomorrow."

Uncle Harry left the meat counter and walked up to the front, still holding a butcher knife. His apron was stained with blood. "Where'd you come from?" he said.

That was none of his business, but the stranger didn't take offense. "Shreveport, last stop. Working my way west. Been hitching rides, decided to stop here and look for work. You know anybody needs odd jobs done, or farm work?"

The girls hiding behind the makeup shelf giggled and shushed each other, except for Wanda Patterson, who looked directly at the man and smiled. Uncle Harry's eyes narrowed. His frown told me he was about to say "No," like he always does when men from outside talk about hanging around, but before he could say anything, Old Brother Fisher, who always tried to help people, slapped down a domino and called out, "Try the Conrad place. Frank Conrad owns several hundred acres the other side of the river. Heard him say the other day he needs some fences repaired, and three of his hands got caught in the draft and left for the Army. Bet he'd take you on. Might keep you to haul hay, maybe pick cotton."

The stranger raised the Coke bottle and nodded at the old man. "Much obliged, sir."

"Go up the road about a half mile to where there's a gap in the fence on the left. Go on through—it's private property, but nobody'll care—and follow the old wagon ruts down to the river. Cross the footbridge. Other side belongs to Conrad. Big white house at the top of the hill."

The stranger picked up his suitcase and started toward the door. Every eye followed him.

"Wait," I said. The eyes all looked my way. "What's your name?"

He turned around and smiled right at me. Just at me. "Campbell. Campbell Reed. What's yours?"

"I'm Rosemary."

"I'm pleased to meet you, Miss Rosemary." Still smiling, he pushed through the screen door and was gone.

Uncle Harry grabbed my arm and jerked me around to face him. "What have I told you about talking to strange men? That one's trouble. Leave him alone."

I pulled away and ran through the storeroom and out the back door, past Uncle Harry's house and the outbuildings, up the footpath and onto the gravel bar that lay along a stretch of the river bank. Wading in to where the water was clear, I bent down and splashed some on my cheeks, then straightened up and let the slight breeze cool my face. I was fifteen years old, and I'd had enough of Uncle Harry treating me like a baby.

I would stay down here till time for supper. If Uncle Harry wanted me back at the store, he could come find me.

I recognized the looks the men had given Campbell. Except for Old Brother Fisher, they thought the same as Uncle Harry: he was trouble. I knew what Wanda Patterson and her friends thought, too: not trouble, but a good-looking man to take them out on Saturday nights, to park with in the cemetery after dark, to beg their mamas to invite for dinner, and, if they were lucky, to marry and have babies with.

But when I looked at him, I didn't see trouble or fun or babies or anything like that.

In the time it took Campbell Reed to tell me his name, I looked at him and saw a savior.

* * * *

That night at dinner, Uncle Harry started in on me. "I've told you to ignore trash like that. Next time he comes in, keep your mouth shut."

"I was trying to make a customer feel welcome, that's all. When you're polite to a customer, he'll buy more. That's what Aunt Violet said. Anyway, you don't know he's trash."

"I know enough." He finished slicing off a bite of steak and then pointed the knife at me. "He's got the same look in his eye your daddy did when he come slinking around here bothering your mother. He left town the minute she told him he'd got her in trouble."

"Harry, stop," said Aunt Violet. "She doesn't need to hear this again."

"It's time she paid attention."

"Not while you're angry." Aunt Violet put an extra-big piece of buttermilk pie and a clean fork on a plate and handed it to him. "Take your dessert out on the porch."

He got all swelled up, like he did when he was in a pout, but he did what Aunt Violet told him.

After we heard the screen door open and close, she set a slice of pie before me and began taking dishes off the table and stacking them in the sink. I thought she would say something, but she didn't, so I had to ask.

"What do I need to pay attention to?"

She ran water until it was hot and poured soap into the dishpan. "Nothing, really. You have to remember that Harry loved your mother. He wanted to marry her and make you his daughter. When she—went away—he was disappointed. Hurt. You remind him of her. He doesn't want you to make the same mistake."

"Maybe it wasn't a mistake," I said. "Maybe she's having a fine time in New York City or Hollywood or somewhere. Maybe she married some rich man and has everything she ever dreamed of. Maybe leaving me here was the best thing she ever did. Maybe any day now she'll come back and get me."

Aunt Violet ran hot water over a plate and set it upright in the drainer. "That's a nice dream, honey, but I wouldn't depend on it. I'm sure she'd like to come for you, but lots of things can get in the way of doing what we want."

She sounded so sad, like she was thinking of herself instead of me.

"Did something ever get in the way of one of your dreams?"

She stood very still with her back to me, staring out the window into the dusk. I watched her reflection in the glass. She was my mother's younger sister, tall but fragile-looking, with fine blond hair she pulled up into a bun, and pretty, like a woman named Violet ought to be. She was a lot younger than Harry.

She was quiet so long I thought she'd forgotten I was there. But then she came back from wherever she'd been. "Get in the way? Maybe. A long time ago. It doesn't matter now."

She was welcome to think that way if it made her feel better. But my dream mattered. I mattered. And nothing would get in my way.

* * * *

For weeks after that, Uncle Harry made me stay home all day so I wouldn't have a chance to see Campbell. Violet nearly went crazy trying to find jobs for me around the house. There's only so much sweeping and dusting a person can do. She finally sat me down at the sewing machine and put me to making feed sack aprons and kitchen towels for the church bring-and-buy. But after a while, she began to be short with me. I didn't blame her. I guessed she valued her time alone. Anyway, we were running out of feed sacks.

Uncle Harry finally admitted he needed help and let me come back to work, after giving me a lecture about leaving strange men alone. But it appeared Frank Conrad was keeping Campbell too busy on the farm to spend time in town. Aunt Violet said she saw Campbell sometimes when he came in late, when she was at the store counting money and doing the bookkeeping.

But even with Uncle Harry watching me, I managed to talk to Campbell once on the sly. After supper one evening, Aunt Violet had me deliver a casserole to a neighbor whose wife was in the hospital with a new baby. Coming home I took a shortcut across the Conrad place. I'd just crossed the footbridge and started down the path when I nearly stumbled over Campbell Reed, sitting with his back against a cypress tree.

My heart pounded. For a few seconds, I stopped breathing. But I made myself calm down and say hello. He looked up and smiled. "Miss

Rosemary. What are you doing here at this time of the evening?" He was using a pocket knife to cut a small block of wood.

"You whittling?"

"Carving." He held up a small figure. It was a girl's head.

I sat down beside him. "Is that somebody you know?"

"Light's getting too dim." He closed the knife and set it on the ground between us. It was bigger than the one Uncle Harry carried. I reached for it.

"Don't touch that." He grabbed my wrist with one hand, hard, and with the other snatched up the knife.

I pulled back, frightened, and started to jump up. "I'm sorry. I didn't mean—"

His voice softened. "Don't go. I'm not mad. I was afraid you'd hurt yourself. Look." He took the knife by its tortoiseshell handle and held it away from his body, where I could see. Suddenly, like magic, the blade flew out. It glinted in the last rays of the sun. I gasped.

"Switchblade," he said. He showed me a little button on the side of the handle, then closed the blade, held the knife where I could see how it worked, and pushed the button. Again the blade flew out. "You see?" He closed it again and held it out to me.

I shook my head.

"It's okay. Take it. Okay, now hold it steady."

I pressed the button. Smiling, I folded the blade back in until it clicked and handed the knife back. He put it into his pocket and leaned back against the tree. For a while nobody said anything. Finally, I asked.

"You planning to stay here long?"

"Nope. Just long enough to make a little money. I want to buy a set of wheels."

"A what?"

"Set of wheels. A car."

"Where you going when you get 'em?"

"Got my sights set on California."

"Hollywood?"

He shrugged. "Maybe."

"I've always wanted to go to Hollywood. Can I go with you?"

He grinned. "You're sure full of questions, aren't you?"

"Is that bad?"

He stood. "Nope. It's the only way you'll ever learn anything, asking questions." He offered me his hand. I took it. He helped me up.

"Well, Miss Rosemary, it's going to be a long day tomorrow. I've got to get some shut-eye." He put two fingers under my chin and tipped it up. I wondered how those ice-cold eyes could make me feel so warm.

Then he tapped his pocket. "This knife—it'll be our secret."

I nodded.

He walked up the path, crossed the footbridge, and headed across the flat and up the hill. The half-carved figure of the girl's head lay on the ground where he'd left it. I picked it up and traced its surface with my finger. It looked a little bit like me.

The knife was our secret. There was another secret, too, that only I knew. But one day soon it would belong to both of us.

* * * *

Not long after, something happened to set the whole town talking. Campbell Reed showed up at church. He wore a suit and a white shirt and tie, and he sat beside Francie Conrad. Her mama and daddy sat one pew behind, and acted like they thought Campbell was one of the family.

Mr. and Mrs. Conrad didn't socialize in town, but they knew people's names and were friendly enough in the churchyard after services. But Francie Conrad had nothing in common with people on the town side of the river, and she didn't pretend otherwise. Town girls wore homemade dresses and went to the local school. Francie bought a new wardrobe in Dallas every year and went to school in the East. Town girls joined 4-H and Future Homemakers; Francie belonged to a sorority. She was perfect—her skin, her hair, her clothes—but she was set apart. She had no one to whisper secrets to, no one to share her dreams. In that way, she and I were alike.

But we were different, too, because what Francie wanted, she got. If Frank Conrad let her sit in church with one of his hired hands, she must have wanted that hired hand awfully bad.

At Sunday dinner that day, Uncle Harry started in carping about Campbell Reed, calling him "trash" and "no-account," the same words he'd been spouting all summer. He said Campbell was playing up to Conrad and this proved he was just out for whatever he could get.

Aunt Violet shook her head, but gently. "No-accounts don't show up at church on Sunday. The minister said Campbell wants to be baptized."

"Preachers'll believe anybody that says they want to be baptized. The devil would get baptized if he thought it would get him into Francie Conrad's pants."

Aunt Violet's head came up, and she looked across the table with her eyes blazing. "Mind your tongue. I won't have that kind of language in front of Rosemary."

"There's some facts of life she'd better get straight, the sooner the better, and that's one of them. Men'll tell you whatever you want to hear to get what they want. And most women are silly enough to let them have it."

"Harry, you don't know one thing about women."

"And I guess you know all about men?"

Aunt Violet's cheeks turned a blotchy pink.

"I'm doing what fathers are supposed to do," said Uncle Harry, "watching over their daughters. Taking care they don't fall prey to men with dishonorable intentions. Teaching them what men are like, that you can't depend on none of them."

"Including you?" I said.

"Rosemary, we'll have no backtalk. Apologize to your uncle." Aunt Violet's voice was quiet, but after I mumbled, "I'm sorry," she turned back to Uncle Harry like I'd never said a word.

"Well, then. I guess by your standards, Frank Conrad's taking care of his daughter just fine, having her and Campbell in church right there right under his nose. Conrad must think well of the young man, letting him sit in the family pew where everybody can see him, keeping him on the payroll, selling him a car. If things go all right, Campbell might even settle down here."

"Hmmph. Conrad sold that boy a car hoping he'll jump in and take off when nobody's looking. He better take care Francie don't jump in and take off with him. Or that he don't run off and leave her with a little present she can't get rid of."

Harry'd started out talking about Francie and Campbell Reed, but now he was talking about me. I'd been a little present. But my mama managed to get rid of me. When I was a baby, she ran off, leaving me with Aunt Violet.

"That's enough, Harry," said Aunt Violet. "I'm tired of listening to you. Either change the subject or take your plate and get out of here."

Uncle Harry took a couple more bites of pot roast and mashed potatoes. Then he got up and stormed off toward the living room.

Aunt Violet threw her napkin on the table and stood. "Rosemary, leave the dishes. I'll clean up the kitchen later." She pushed through the screen door and let it slam behind her.

I cleared the table and started water running in the sink. I didn't mind. Washing and drying dishes gave me time to think. And I had plenty to think about.

Aunt Violet was right: Uncle Harry didn't know a thing about women, least of all me. Last year, when he found me sneaking in the back door at midnight, he thought I was going out to meet boys, and he took to locking me in my bedroom every night. But it was easy as pie to go out the window and climb down the oak tree. I could get out whenever

I wanted. Not to meet boys, though. There wasn't a boy in town who interested me, and I wasn't going to settle.

If you asked me, Frank Conrad wasn't taking as good care of Francie as Aunt Violet thought. Because on the nights her high-class girlfriends came visiting, or weekends when she was in Dallas with her mother, shopping, I was sitting in the crotch of a tree down on the river, watching Campbell Reed escort Wanda Patterson along the footpath and up to the abandoned cabin on the old Timmerman place.

It seemed like, without even looking their way, Campbell had known those girls were watching him in the store that day, just praying for him to make a move. And that none of them was going to tell him, "No."

So all those weeks, when Uncle Harry thought I was in bed asleep, I sat in the tree and watched and waited.

Then one Saturday morning, just as we were getting ready to open the store, Old Brother Fisher came running in, all out of breath, hollering for Uncle Harry to call the sheriff. He'd gone to the river to run his trotlines and found a body floating face down in the water, caught between his boat and the roots of a cypress tree. It was Wanda Patterson. Her throat had been cut from ear to ear.

* * * *

After they found Wanda, Uncle Harry really came down hard on me. He watched me all day and wouldn't let me out in the evenings, not even to feed the barn cats. He took care of my outside chores. And he told me in no uncertain terms not to go down to the river.

The day before, being barred from the river would have been like being in prison. I'd have been so angry, I'd have run down there as soon as his back was turned. But after they found Wanda, I didn't argue.

So at night, I lay on my bed, thinking about Campbell, wondering what he was doing, whether he was taking anyone else to the old house. I wondered whether any girl would go with him. I wondered whether Francie would want him now.

It wasn't long before I heard about Francie. The town grapevine made sure of that. Almost before Wanda's body was pulled out of the river, Frank Conrad put his wife and daughter on an airplane to New York City. From there, Francie would go on to Switzerland for a year in finishing school. No one said whether she cried and carried on, pleading with her daddy to let her stay with Campbell, or whether she was so afraid of getting her throat cut, she wanted to leave, maybe even begged to get on that plane.

No matter how Francie felt, people on the town side of the river were scared. The sheriff questioned Campbell, just like he questioned all the boys Wanda had run around with, but he let them go. He refused to name a suspect, said whoever did it was smart enough not to leave much evidence. I overheard a deputy tell Uncle Harry they didn't have any evidence at all. People got nervous. They wanted somebody locked up so they could forget about Wanda and get on with their lives.

Uncle Harry helped them out by choosing his own suspect. He hung about on the sidewalk in front of the store and collared everybody who walked by. Their tongues itched to gossip. Conversations that started with "Maybe" ended with "That's a fact," and in that way every word they said became evidence in the court of public opinion. Those inclined to be fair shook their heads at what the world was coming to and disengaged themselves from Uncle Harry as soon as possible. But all of them remembered what he'd said.

It didn't take long for words to turn into deeds. People who used to stop and pass the time of day with Campbell now nodded and kept walking. People who used to nod now crossed the street when they saw him coming. He moved from the Conrads' church pew to a seat in the very back. After the benediction, he was the first one out the door. He didn't stay to visit, just sort of disappeared.

And no matter what the town thought of Campbell Reed, one fact wouldn't go away: Wanda Patterson was dead. And whoever killed her was still out there carrying a knife.

Old Brother Fisher said that one evening when he was setting out trotlines, he saw Campbell sitting on the river bank. He said he told Campbell it'd be best to stay away from there, all things considered, because even an innocent man could look like he was guilty. "Might be best," he said, "if he just packed up and left before folks here get any more ideas."

When Uncle Harry heard that, he snorted. "Don't need more ideas to know what's what. The guilty always return to the scene of the crime. He is waiting for another innocent young girl to come by."

Uncle Harry didn't know I'd made up my mind to be that girl.

* * * *

When I got to the river that evening, Campbell was sitting in the same place he'd been before, carving a new block of wood.

"You shouldn't be here." He stabbed the knife blade into the ground. "Aren't you afraid of me?"

"No."

He laughed. "Then you're the only one."

"You didn't kill her." I sat down beside him. "You wouldn't kill anyone. The sheriff didn't say you killed her."

He looked away. "Yeah. But it doesn't make any difference. People have me tried and convicted. Only thing left is the execution, and I wouldn't put it past them to get up a lynch mob. There are some good hanging trees down here."

I gasped. "Then you better leave. Just pack up and go. Tonight. Don't give them a chance to catch you." *Don't let Uncle Harry catch you*, is what I was thinking.

"I'm going, all right. The car's about ready. Got to replace the windshield wipers and give it a good wash and wax. It's a nice set of wheels. Won't be long and I'll be on my way." When he said this, he was watching the river flowing by, reflecting the reds and golds of sunset. But now he turned his head and looked directly into my eyes. "You're a sweet girl, Rosemary, to care about what happens to me."

Finally it was time for me to speak. "Take me with you. I can be ready tonight. I'll sneak out. They'll never know where we've gone."

Campbell sat forward and opened his mouth like he wanted to say something, but I didn't let him.

"I have money saved up from working in the store. Not much, but it'll help buy gasoline and food. And when we get where we're going, I'll get a job, a real one, and help pay rent and things. And if you don't want to go to Hollywood, that's okay, I'll go anywhere with you, if you'll just let me."

I held my breath, waiting.

One corner of his mouth curved up, but his forehead wrinkled, like he was trying to figure something out. "Like I said, you're a sweet girl to care, and that's a generous offer, but I can't take you with me. It's not—"

"But I do care about you. I love you. And I'll do anything you want, anything." I threw my arms around his neck and kissed him.

He pushed me away. "Stop it." He tried to grab my wrists, but I kissed him again, and all of a sudden his arms were around me and he was kissing me back, real kisses, and then we were lying together on the grass, just him and me under the trees and the sky and the sun going down into the water. I unbuttoned his shirt and began unbuttoning my blouse, but then something changed, and he got his hands on my shoulders and pushed me off him. He got up and walked away and then stopped and looked back at me, sitting on the ground. I scrambled to my feet but he shouted at me.

"Don't move, Rosie. Stay right there." He was breathing fast. He buttoned his shirt. Then he walked back to where he'd left his knife and pulled it out of the ground.

"What did I do?" I said. "Why are you mad at me?"

He sighed. "I'm not mad at you, I'm mad at me. Look. We can't ever do that again, you hear? And I can't take you to California or anywhere else."

"Why? You could if you wanted to."

He stood there for a moment, flicking bits of grass and dirt off the blade. When he spoke, his voice was as cold as his eyes. "Well, I don't want to. You're just a kid."

I clenched my fists. "I'm not a kid."

"You're a baby." He walked away. "So go home. It's past your bed-time."

I ran at him, pounded his back with my fists. He turned and, with one hand, pushed me away so hard I fell backwards. I began to cry.

"See? You're boo-hooing like a baby. Now get out of here before I do something I'll regret."

I looked up. He stood over me holding the knife. Then, making a sound deep in his throat, he folded the blade and threw it toward the river. It made a chinking sound when it hit the gravel bar.

I picked myself up and ran to the house. The television was on in the living room. Tiptoeing past the door, I saw Uncle Harry dozing in his chair. I sneaked up the stairs to my room, flung myself face down on the bed, and sobbed.

After a while I calmed down. I got up and took a bath, put on paja-mas, and got into bed. I wasn't going to let anyone hear me crying into my pillow over Campbell Reed.

But later, the front door opening woke me. Aunt Violet was coming in from choir practice. She rattled around in the kitchen for a few min-utes, then started up the stairs. Those few minutes were enough time for me to remember what Campbell had said. The wound was raw, and the pain surged back like new. Again I began to sob.

Then Aunt Violet was standing beside my bed. "Rosemary? What's the matter?"

I couldn't tell her. "You're late."

"I stayed behind for a few minutes. Somebody needed to talk to me. Now what happened to make you cry, baby? Tell me."

Baby, she called me. But nice. Not like he'd had said it.

"Campbell." The pillow muffled my words. "I want to go away with him, but he won't take me."

Aunt Violet slipped off her shoes and lay down beside me. "Put your head on my shoulder." She wrapped her arms around me and stroked my hair and let me cry myself out.

"I think I understand," she said. "It's hard when your dream doesn't come true."

That started me crying again, but not for long. I didn't have any tears left.

"One day you *will* leave, but not with a man who's just passing through. I've saved a little money, and I'll save more, so you can go to business school, maybe even college, and then find a good job."

"But how? Uncle Harry says there's never any extra money. How much do you have?"

"I've put away some of my sewing money, and egg money, and other bits I picked up. Just a dollar or two, here and there. But I've been saving since you were a baby. By the time you're out of school, there'll be enough. You won't live here forever, and you'll be able to take care of yourself, and never have to depend on anyone else, ever, except the people you choose."

I thought about the day Campbell arrived, when I asked a question Aunt Violet didn't answer. I asked it again. "Has anything ever gotten in the way of your dream coming true?"

She was quiet so long, I thought she wouldn't answer this time either. "When I was just about your age, a boy came to town. He was older, closer to your mama's age. She already had you and she loved you, but when he left, she went with him."

"And so you married Harry?"

"Harry had always loved your mama, but she didn't love him back. When she left I think he went a little crazy. Then your grandma died, and Harry knew I needed help, and you were your mama's little girl, so he loved you. And he proposed, and I married him."

"Uncle Harry loved me?"

"Still does. Just doesn't know how to show it. He thinks keeping you cooped up is right. I've told him it doesn't work that way, but he's bringing you up the best way he knows how. Try to remember that when he fusses at you."

I was getting sleepy, lying here with Aunt Violet talking softly, explaining things I'd never understood. I had a million questions, but I was so sleepy, I almost drifted off. Then I remembered.

"What about your dream?"

"Oh, that. Well, it was a long time ago. But… the boy I mentioned? I thought he was my beau. He'd said that when he got ready to leave town, he would take me with him. But he took your mama instead."

I couldn't believe it. All these years, telling me things about my mama, and she'd never said a word about this.

"Didn't you hate Mama for going off like that? And leaving me for you to raise?"

"No, never. Your mama had always been—different. Fragile. She couldn't breathe in this town. If she'd stayed here and married Harry, she would have died. Or someone else would have."

"What about the boy? Going like that without saying good-bye. Did you hate him?"

She sighed. "Hate's a strong word. I learned not to think about him."

After that, there was nothing left to say. I felt so bad for her, I wanted to say something to make her feel better. But I was too tired from crying to think. I was almost asleep when Aunt Violet said one more thing.

"What you have to remember about dreams, baby, is that they take time. You don't give up. For dreams to come true, you have to wait."

* * * *

When I woke the next morning, the sun was making a crisscross pattern on my window shades. I'd never slept this late. I jumped up and threw on my clothes. Aunt Violet would be helping Uncle Harry, and she needed to be home working on her sewing. I ran downstairs and all the way to the store.

I knew Uncle Harry would be mad, so I slowed down and slipped through the door, trying to escape attention. But he didn't even look up. He was sitting at the domino table. Old Brother Fisher stood beside him, patting him on the shoulder. Other people stood around, looking serious, talking in whispers. Some of the women were crying.

I walked over to the table.

He looked up. "She's gone. Run off with that Campbell Reed." He handed me the letter she'd left for him. "What are we going to do, Rosemary? What will we do without Violet?"

I set the letter back on the table and walked out. Back in my bedroom, I sat on the bed. The woman's head that Campbell had been carving on the riverbank that first night we talked looked at me from the nightstand. I picked it up and traced its features with my finger.

It had long, curling hair and lips that curved into a gentle smile, and eyes that gazed into the distance. It didn't look a thing like me.

It looked like Aunt Violet.

* * * *

I was sitting in the front porch swing, reading, when a dark blue convertible rolled up the dusty drive and parked beside the house. A man got out. Campbell Reed.

He closed the door and stood beside the car. "It's been a long time."

Three years. Time enough for me to finish school. Time enough to learn that the money Aunt Violet had saved came from taking a little at a time from the store receipts when she did the books. Time enough for Uncle Harry to have a stroke and die.

Three years for Campbell Reed to return to scene of the crime.

I closed the book and walked to the top of the steps. "You must be doing well for yourself. That's a nice set of wheels."

He laughed. "Better than that heap I left here in. I guess Violet wrote and told you I was coming. She's got the money to start you in school out there. So pack your bags. We're heading west."

"They're already packed."

Aunt Violet had written every week since she got to California. She wrote about her new job, her apartment, her neighbors. But one thing she didn't write about, and I needed to know.

"Are you and Aunt Violet married?"

He shook his head. "Violet never cared for me that way. She wanted out of here. I was just transportation." He walked to the back of the car and opened the trunk. "You told anybody you're leaving?"

"Two or three." I'd put the property in the hands of a realtor, like Aunt Violet instructed. The neighbor who'd been running the store while I was in school was interested in buying it. I'd told the preacher I was taking the bus to see Aunt Violet. It seemed the less said about Campbell, the better.

"If you're ready, I'd as soon get on the road right now. There are people in this town I'd rather not run into."

He followed me inside and picked up my bags. I'd gotten rid of most of my things. Aunt Violet had said my old clothes wouldn't do, and I could buy new ones when I got there.

"You want to go down to the river before we leave?"

Campbell arranged the bags in the trunk and slammed it closed. "Sure. I'm willing to risk it if you are. Get in. We'll drive down the road and park on the Timmerman place. Don't want anyone spotting the car here in front of the house and decide to get nosy."

"I'd rather walk. I'll meet you there."

"Suit yourself." The tires made a second set of tracks in the dust. In the west, a bank of thunderclouds was building up, promising a late summer electrical storm. One good downpour would wash the tracks away. No one would even suspect Campbell had been here.

I ran into the house and changed into my bathing suit, stuffed the clothes I'd taken off into a train case, put a rolled-up towel under my arm, and headed for the river.

Campbell was waiting when I got there, standing with his back to me. I picked up a rock and threw it. The plunk when it hit the water startled him. He swung around.

"Bathing suit?"

"I'll take one last dip. Once I leave here, I won't be coming back." I held up the train case. "Don't worry. I've got clothes. I won't get your upholstery all wet."

I ran to the water's edge and set the case down at the base of a willow tree growing out of the bank. Then I dove in, swam to the other side and back, ducked under, and came up shaking water out of my hair. Just last week I'd had it cut almost as short as a boy's. It would dry in no time.

I swam once more across and back, then got out and, picking up the towel, walked onto the bank to where Campbell sat against the same tree where we'd talked that night three years before.

Setting the towel on the grass, I wondered whether he'd ever regretted taking Violet instead of me.

He looked up. His eyes were the same icy blue. "I like your hair."

"I had it cut last week. There was a picture of a movie actress in the newspaper with hair like this."

"Makes you look like a movie actress. Older."

"Just turned eighteen. I'm not a baby anymore."

"No, you're not." He took my hand and pulled me down beside him. "I've thought about you, you know. I'm sorry about how it turned out. But I couldn't take you with me."

"I know." I shouldn't have been surprised. Uncle Harry was right. Men are like that. You can't depend on them.

He reached over and ran his thumb across my lower lip. "Did you mean what you said that time about loving me? Because I swear, Rosie, it would be real easy to fall in love with you." He leaned toward me. I took his face in my hands and kissed him.

This time he didn't hesitate, but put his arms around me and kissed me back. I freed myself and unbuttoned his shirt. He took it off and then pulled off his T-shirt. I pushed him back onto the grass and stretched out on top of him and kissed him again.

He reached for the straps of my swimsuit. "I've dreamed about this, Rosie."

I pushed his hands away. "Wait. For dreams to come true, you have to wait." I sat up, straddling him, and reached for the towel. "Let me dry off first. I'm getting you all wet."

He put his hands under his head and lay still, watching me. "You trust me, don't you, Rosie? After Wanda was killed, you and Violet were the only ones. Everybody else, even Francie, believed I killed that girl. But you trusted me. You came to meet me down here, right where they'd found her body."

"Of course I trusted you." I unrolled the towel. "I knew you didn't kill her."

"Aw, Rosie, you didn't know me from Adam. How could you be sure I didn't do it?"

"Because I was here."

His black brows drew together, but he kept smiling, like he believed me but wanted me to say it was a joke. "You were where?"

"Here. So I know who did it."

Campbell's smile faded. He still lay with his hands under his head, but now he seemed paralyzed.

From inside the towel, I pulled out the switchblade he'd thrown away the last time we were together.

"I know you didn't kill Wanda Patterson." I turned the knife in my hand and held it just as he'd taught me. "You were mine, not hers. But you would never have killed her. So I killed her myself."

I pressed the button. The blade flashed out.

Campbell's eyes widened. He drew his hands from behind his head, opened his mouth, but before he could touch me, the knife slid smoothly across his throat, cutting off all sound.

* * * *

It was over in no time. Using the towel to soak up the blood, I rolled his body to the edge of the bank and pushed it into deepest pool. Then I ran upstream, dived in, stripped off my suit, and washed myself clean. Hiding among the willow branches, I dressed in the clothes I'd brought in the train case and replaced them with my damp suit.

The knife I slipped into my pocket.

From the top of the hill, I took a last look at the spot where Campbell's body had sunk. There wasn't a trace, not even a ripple. Not one piece of evidence.

I made my way to the abandoned house where Campbell had hidden the car. For a full minute I sat in the driver's seat inhaling the clean, new smell. I'd never driven a new car. I turned the key in the ignition, drove to the highway, and headed west.

The car was smooth, sensitive to my touch. It floated above the asphalt and hugged the curves. Driving it was a dream come true.

Campbell had done all right. It was a nice set of wheels.

FAMILY BUSINESS

REAVIS Z. WORTHAM

Sitting under this shade tree and studying on the yellow wheel of my John Deere tractor, I'm thinking about how wheels have had such an impact on my family up here in the northeast Texas bottomlands.

It all started way back in the Dust Bowl days, when Great-grandpa John Caissen took a notion to quit the whiskey business. It was probably the worst time he could have chosen, but he decided that he was through runnin' from the law. Great-grandpa had it in his head to go back to farming, and right at that moment in time, the idea looked promising. A few well-timed soaking rains had temporarily greened the bottoms and he thought the drought was over.

He was kinda right. There was enough moisture in the ground to make a fair-to-middlin' corn crop that year. Family and friends came together during harvest to celebrate. My dad was there, but he wasn't much more than six or seven. Stalk after stalk, row after row, they picked corn, twisting each ear free and tossing it into a wagon pulled by a matched set of blue-nosed mules that worked together all day long.

Great-grandpa always preferred mules because they had more sense, were less expensive than horses, and didn't need a lot of fancy feed. They were happy with hay, grass, and a bait of oats every now and then.

He was especially proud of Molly and Jack, particularly on the way home out of the bottoms each day. The team seemed to know when they were being watched. No matter how tired they were, the mules raised their heads, perked their ears, and trotted past the loafers at the old country store like a couple of high-bred Tennessee Walkers.

A lot of folks tried to buy that team from Great-grandpa, but he never even studied on the idea. Those two were like family and had belonged to him since they were foals. He'd used them for years to plow the family garden, to pull stumps and logs, and to haul firewood from places where cars and trucks couldn't go. They were a good team and seemed to enjoy the work.

They let him down that one day, though.

Mules don't spook easily, and they seldom panic, but the buzz of a rattlesnake scares any living thing that draws a breath. It was a big one laying in the middle of the cornfield, and when he rattled, people scattered in all directions. Molly and Jack jerked in the harness, rolling their eyes and snorting at the dry warning of danger. They stomped across the rows, threatening to take off through the unharvested half of the field.

Great-grandpa John was close enough that he tried to jump on the wagon to catch the reins. He would have made it, too, if a cornstalk hadn't tripped him up just as he sprang for the seat. The wooden hub of the front wheel slammed against his thigh, knocking him ass over teakettle. He fell in a sprawl. The wheel weighed heavy by a half load of corn ran over that same thigh, nearly severing his leg.

From what I've heard through the years, that old man was cut from aged oak, and hard enough to bend a sharp sixteen-gauge nail if someone was to try and drive one in him. He didn't holler much, and they say it didn't look too bad at first glance because the soft, faded denim of his old bib overalls hid the wound. That is, until blood started pouring out and wouldn't stop.

His oldest son, Web, was there, along with half a dozen other hard-working folks. Web tied a belt around the thigh, and some of the men held Great-grandpa's leg so it wouldn't fall off when they picked him up and put him in an empty wagon waiting in the shade of an oak. The old man cussed all the way home while Web beat their friend's team of borrowed mules to a foam.

Old Doc Bailey showed up about an hour later. Like most country doctors of the time, he was blunt. "I'm afraid your leg's done for, John."

Great-grandpa John was still in his right mind at that point, but barely. "I believe you're right. Well, go ahead on and take it off. We'll see what happens after that." Then he drank a quart of his own diminishing stock of homemade whiskey and Doc Bailey went to work on the mangled leg, but the damage was too great. Blood loss and trauma did him in.

After paying for the funeral, the crop barely brought in enough to even up their grocery bill at the store.

Out of money the next year, Grandpa Web gave up on farming and went straight back into the moonshine business to make some real cash. He dug the copper line and boiler out of the ditch behind Great-grandpa's house, and a month later started selling what folks said was the smoothest whiskey that ever came out of Lamar County. It was so pure, when customers shook the jar, folks said the tiny bubbles reminded them of champagne.

Oh, he wasn't making a killing off the profits and getting rich or nothin', but as the Depression years passed, the Caissens weren't living on beans and cornbread like lots of other families in the bottoms. They were doing all right when others could barely scrape up two nickels to rub together.

World War II brought a boom. Grandpa Web added more stills in the bottoms and sold whiskey in a steady flow to the thousands of thirsty servicemen coming through Camp Maxey, just north of Paris.

There was always danger in making whiskey, and moonshiners spent a considerable amount of time running from deputies, constables, and revenuers. The Caissens got caught sometimes, and first one still then another was shut down, but my people always paid their way out of jail and hid another boiler even deeper in the woods. It was a fine life full of adventure and excitement, and despite the war, things were good until them sorry Red River County boys, Bill Nichols and Cecil Whip, set up shop in the next county and tried to horn in.

First they tried to buy Grandpa Web out, but he wasn't having none of it. They tried muscle next, but that didn't work either, so Bill and Cecil resorted to shooting Grandpa with a twelve-gauge up at our little country store.

We don't know for sure who pulled the trigger, but the shooter missed as their car slowed on the highway. How you can miss with a shotgun still mystifies me, but he did. They got away, but Grandpa Web found out who done it, and when Cecil stepped out of his outhouse a week later, he walked right into a full load of number four buckshot.

It didn't do to cross the son of John Caissen.

A month later, a fisherman on the Red River felt a strange weight in his illegal net and found Bill Nichols tangled up with a couple of bass and a big old shovelnose catfish. Nobody could recognize Bill right off, because the fish and turtles had been at him for a while, but the sheriff remembered a blurry anchor tattooed on Bill's forearm and identified him by that. They put Bill on ice, and took the fisherman to the hoosegow.

By the time the Japs surrendered and the government closed down most of the army camp, the Caissens thought that little hometown feud was over. They figured what was left of the Red River County crew would stay on their side of the line, and our kinfolk on ours.

They were wrong.

Times were harder once all the soldiers left and the boom ended. The Red River boys got hungry and once again decided to eliminate the competition… that is, Grandpa Web.

This time their new boss, Jimmy Ray Whip, took over. He was Cecil's baby brother and back from the army with a little trick he'd learned as a demolition expert. He wired a couple of sticks of dynamite to the ignition of Grandpa Web's car. Wouldn't you know it? It wasn't Grandpa who hit the starter on that cold November morning in 1946, but a shade-tree mechanic named R.D. Jenkins, who was fixin' to take Grandpa's car to his house and rebuild the engine.

Grandpa was standing on the porch with a cup of coffee in his hand when ol' R.D. and the DeSoto pretty well vaporized. It didn't help, Grandpa being on the porch and all. One of the hubcaps shot across the yard like a Frisbee and took Grandpa Web's head clean off.

Grandpa Web had a son, and that was Dad, who was eating breakfast in the kitchen at the time. The concussion blew out all the windows, but he didn't even get a scratch, though there was glass and blood all in his cornbread and sweet milk.

Dad dropped out of high school and retreated to the safety of Alabama kinfolk for a while. It was there he learned to drive as blocker for a different kind of moonshiner. Those Alabama wild men took bootlegging to an entirely different level, and that's where Dad found his calling as a driver.

Back then, the blocker drove ahead of a delivery vehicle full of whiskey to draw attention to themselves. When the laws saw the speeding car, they took off after it like a house afire, sometimes drawing more than one police car into the chase.

With the police concentrating on a guy speeding around in a souped-up sedan, the delivery car simply moseyed on down the road, not worrying about getting stopped to see why the rear end was sitting so low on a family car, or to look under the tarp on the back of a truck.

Dad did that for a few years, until he came back to Lamar County with a new idea to put the Red River bunch out of business once and for all. He set up two stills down deep in the woods, brought in half a dozen trusted (and hard-barked) family members, and went to work building the business back up to where it had been in the thirties and early forties.

Dad was second cousin with the new sheriff in Red River County. He dropped by the courthouse with a wad of bills big enough to choke a horse and left it on Cousin Sheriff's desk, with the understanding that there was more to come if the Red River bunch was to find themselves in a shallow grave, or the pen.

And wouldn't you know it? Two months later, a right smart number Whips and Nichols turned up dead. Them that survived, and that included Jimmy Ray Whip, had their mail delivered to the Walls unit down in Huntsville.

It wasn't long before Dad's new business was running smooth as clockwork. He graduated from driving the whiskey himself, to hiring it done. His crew was professional, and they handled everything from buying the supplies to delivery. Dad built a modest two-story on a hill overlooking the river bottoms, bought some bottomland, and went to farming cotton, corn, and eventually soybeans. As the cash rolled in from the whiskey, he plowed that illegitimate money into the ground and when the crop sold, it went into the bank as clean cash.

The Caissens were once again in high-cotton, as they used to say.

But Dad never lost his love of driving fast after those Alabama years. He even drove us to and from church so fast it looked like we were trying to outrun the old Devil hisself with that rooster-tail of dust rising high behind our sedan. It didn't have to be cars, though, for him to get that taste of speed. Dad drove the dog-water out of an old 1948 Ford step-side pickup that was a leftover from the good ol' days. Folks often talked about it shooting down the highway like a rocket.

Like ol' vaporized R.D., Dad was also a great shade-tree mechanic, and could tear an engine down on Saturday morning for a ring job, and have it back together in time to drive into town that same night for the evening street dance.

He taught me how to drive it in the river bottoms, on the dirt roads between his fields of cotton or corn, but it nearly killed us both when I was learning how to shift the gears. No matter how many times I sat behind the wheel, I couldn't get it through my head when to push the clutch on a shift, or when I needed to brake.

One day we were moving along at a right smart clip, with a big rooster-tail of dust blowing up behind us. I was pretty proud of myself for driving, and couldn't take my eyes off the rearview mirror and the cloud of dirt that boiled up and then drifted across the fields.

The old man was pretty calm at first. He just shifted his chew to the opposite cheek so he could talk better. "Slow down, son. We're coming up on a curve."

When I saw the hard left turn coming up on us so fast, my mind went to mush.

Dad saw it too. "Said slow down."

I let off the foot-feed and pushed in on the clutch, but forgot the brake. We slowed, some, but not enough. Dad reached over with his big old hand, and grabbed the wheel. He shoved it and the truck slewed to the right just in time to miss a lightning-struck pecan tree that would have split us down the middle like a meat clever. We hit something in the tall Johnson grass and the front fender went sailing away like a wounded quail fluttering in the air.

That broke me free and I stomped the brake. We slid to a stop and the pickup jerked a couple of times and died.

Dad sat back and ran his fingers through his wavy red hair. He leaned out to spit a long brown stream, and then grinned. "I believe we need to practice some more out in that big meadow of hay grazer."

So I learned to drive in a five hundred acre field of alfalfa and became part of the business, hauling whiskey for the old man.

He taught my baby brother, Tommy Lee, to drive that same truck with similar intentions. Tommy Lee was just like Dad. He was a natural-born mechanic who could fix anything. He loved speed, too, which is how we lost him in 1988 when he replaced the '48's original six cylinder engine with a V-8. Tommy Lee dropped that motor in on Saturday morning, and was haul-assin' down Highway 271 to deliver a load of white lightning to a big distributer we used in Oklahoma.

The highway patrol estimates that when the right front tire blew out and caused the steering to fail, Tommy Lee Caissen must have been going about a hundred and twenty in a forty-year-old truck designed for farm work.

The highway patrol told a local newspaper reporter that he was impressed with Dad's truck. "Hell, the bearings on those wheels must have been made out of some space age material. They were still spinning when we got there, and didn't stop for fifteen minutes after. I never saw nothin' like it."

Dad drove up five minutes after the wheel quit spinning round. That one was hard for the old man, because he blamed himself for Tommy Lee's death. We all told him the only fault lay with my brother using a farm truck like a race car, but Dad didn't see it that way.

He blamed the whiskey, because that's what was in the bed, and said enough was enough. He shut down the stills, sold the copper and boilers, and our family went to farming full time. After that, it was corn, soybeans, and marijuana. That last little cash crop sold better, made more money, and was perfect for folks who knew about agriculture.

Why did that pop into my mind on this bright, cool autumn morning, looking at my John Deere upside down in the bar ditch? Well, it's like this. I read once where Robert Todd Lincoln, President Abe Lincoln's son, was cursed. He had breakfast with his dad the morning before he was assassinated in Ford's Theater. In fact, they tried to get Robert to join them for the show that night.

Sixteen years later President Garfield invited Robert to accompany him to the President's college reunion in New Jersey. Robert was late, and arrived only seconds after Garfield was assassinated. The poor bastard wasn't done yet, though.

In 1901, President McKinley invited Robert to attend the Pan-American Exposition with him in New York. Robert got to the expo minutes after the President was shot and killed. Robert was there for three presidents' deaths, more or less, and after that he never wanted to meet another one.

Thinking about how so many of my kinfolk died because of the family business, it's gonna be the same for Dad as it was for Robert Todd Lincoln. He's watched one after another Caissen go on to their rewards.

I forgot my water jug this morning. Even though he's eighty-seven, Dad still gets around pretty good, so he'll see it on the kitchen table and bring it to me. Because of that, he'll be a part of what happened today, and it'll follow him to his grave, probably sooner now than later.

No, I wasn't driving fast, and it wasn't my fault the tractor rolled. That fault lies on the other side of this dirt road, where a black Ford Explorer is wrapped around a red oak tree.

I was just coming up to that old plank bridge over there, heading for the field, when that sorry son-of-a-bitch Chris Whip steered the Explorer around me and tried to pass. Let me tell you, he was a-flyin' and I think he intended to run me into the ditch to set things up for this new century of ours. Him and some of these other dumb bastards around here have started making crystal meth. They should have stayed with corn whiskey, or grass. Those two products are safer by far, and have a proven track record that won't kill the customers.

But when he shot past, the driver's side wheels slipped off the bridge and he lost control. He was trying to compensate for the slide when his back bumper kissed the front of the tractor and knocked me sideways into the bar ditch.

Tractors are like tricycles. When you get them overbalanced on an incline, they'll roll pretty quick, which is what mine did.

Just before I went over, out of the corner of my eye, I saw the Explorer hit the tree and explode. Not with fire like you see on television. It exploded in a cloud of dust, fiberglass, and the contents of the car. You wouldn't believe how much dust is in a live tree, either. When Chris hit the oak, dust flowed down and out like someone shook out a lint mop.

Containers of anhydrous ammonia flew everywhere. A couple of them ruptured and hissed empty in a low-lying fog that's still hanging over the rows. Others scattered on the dirt road and in the field like unexploded bombs. We use anhydrous as liquid fertilizer these days, but that wasn't why they were in the Explorer. Meth cookers mix it with a few things such as battery acid, drain cleaner, and paint thinner to make meth. Better living through chemistry, right?

Chris was probably high as a kite on his own product to begin with, carrying that load of supplies to his trailer down by the creek. I can see him laying there in the dirt, and he ain't moved since he quit plowing with his head.

I'll never know, though, because my tractor wheel that's been spinning all this time is slowing down, and so am I.

It's kinda nice sitting here in this shade as a cool breeze moves the late season grass. I'm disappointed that I won't be in the woods next week after the first freeze to watch the leaves fall. That's one of my favorite things to do, you know.

But I guess this circle of life continues. Or Wheel of Death is more like it.

I drug myself to this tree, after the tractor rolled over on me. My chest feels really squishy and I think a lot of things aren't in their right places anymore. I believe the Red River boys have killed me, and most likely didn't intend to.

Ain't it something that so many of us Caissens were done in by wheels?

At least one thing is funny in all this, though. From where I am, I can see the personalized rear license plate on the stolen Explorer.

It reads, WHEELZ.

ROTA FORTUNAE

V. P. CHANDLER

Tim Brooks listened to the waves as they slapped against the wooden hull of the merchant ship bound for America and wondered if he had made the right decision to stow aboard the *Rota Fortunae*.

I can't be a clerk for the rest of my life! I'm fourteen, old enough to make my own way. I'm sure Uncle Preston could find something for me in Charleston.

He shifted in his cramped hiding space and his stomach growled. He couldn't stand being in the hold any longer. He tentatively poked his head above some barrels. To his left, a chain clinked and Tim let out a shriek.

A pair of bright green eyes caught the sunlight that filtered through the floorboards from above. The eyes stared at him, unmoving.

From above Tim heard, "Did you hear that?" followed by all sorts of lively curses. At that moment Tim doubted whether stowing away to America was a good plan. He didn't know what was more frightening, the men above or whatever was in the hold with him.

The hatch flung open and men peered down.

A voice from somewhere on deck barked, "Well, Peters, what is it?"

A man with a hook of a nose, said, "Cap'n, we got us a young stow-away, a lad. Should we flog 'im?" Enthusiastic cheers answered and more eager faces crowded the hatch and looked down on Tim.

Tim looked around, frantic to find an escape or a weapon.

A voice boomed. "All right, all right, it *has* been some time since we've had a good flogging. Go down and get him." Once again, cheers broke out among the men.

Peters turned his face to the captain. "Begging your pardon, sir, I'll not be the one to go down there, not by meself."

"Do as you're told!"

Peters scurried down the steps and into the hold.

Tim froze like a mouse in front of a cat.

The chains on his left clinked again as a man stood. He was unlike anyone Tim had ever seen. He was at least a head taller than most and his bright green eyes seemed at odds with his dark brown skin. Tim had seen people with dark skin around London, but none that looked as strange and exotic as this mountain of a man. He was so tall, he couldn't stand to his full height in the cramped hold and his long black hair matted together to make strange braids down to his shoulders. The man looked fierce and primitive. Even the chains on his wrists and ankles did not diminish his dignity. The man faced Peters and Tim saw, peeking above the man's collar, a strange tattoo touching his throat. Tim shivered.

Peters looked at Tim. "Come on, lad, time to get on deck."

Tim crawled over the tops of the barrels then stopped. "I… I just want to go to America. My uncle lives there. I'll work for my passage."

"Come on, step to it, boy! I don't want to be in the hold with this heathen, and neither do you."

Tim scrambled over and around barrels, staying as far away from the prisoner as possible. He scurried up the steps, uncertain of his fate.

His eyes adjusted to the light and he assessed the motley crew.

"So, you think you can steal aboard my ship with no consequence?"

Tim turned and faced a man of average height, well-groomed, who looked every part the respectable captain, even down to the knife strapped to his side.

"That's right, lad, I'm Captain Claymore, and who are you?"

"Tim, Tim Preston, sir."

The captain smiled. "Men, we have a lad here with manners. That's good! But maybe he still needs to be taught a lesson?"

A dark man stepped forward. "Captain, I could use an extra pair of hands in the galley." The man held the captain's gaze. The crew became quiet.

"Can you now?" He broke the gaze and looked at Tim. "You're lucky that Spoon needs an extra pair of hands." He motioned to Spoon. "Take him and see to it that he doesn't poison us. Back to work, men!"

The men grumbled and dispersed, but everyone paused when they heard a groan.

Tim followed the sound and saw a pallid-faced man emerging from the forecastle.

"Ohh, ohh, my head. Why am I on a ship?" His clothes were those of a professional man, maybe a banker, not a sailor.

Some of the men smiled.

"I shouldn't be here." He touched the back of his head and winced. "I shouldn't be here. My name is Merrill, I was crimped!"

"Say hey!" replied Peters. "I'm the Boarding Master and I resent that."

"I say, I shouldn't be here! I *need* to be in London today! Don't you see? I was celebrating at a tavern when I was taken. I start a new job today. I *must* be in London!"

Tim wished the man would be quiet. He watched a handful of sailors step closer to Merrill. Tim flashed back to years before, when he witnessed a pack of feral dogs surround a small starving dog in an alley. Back then, he ran away from the growls and yelps. Today he was stuck on a ship in the ocean with nowhere to go.

The captain feigned concern. "Oh, I'm sorry. Peters, this man says he shouldn't be here."

"Begging your pardon, Cap'n. But I got his signature there in the ship's articles."

The captain turned to Merrill and raised his hands. "There you have it. You're in the ship's articles, therefore you are a member of this crew."

"I signed no such papers!"

"Are you calling Peters a liar?"

Merrill looked out upon the ocean. "Surely we're close enough to England to return. I demand you sail back to England!"

Tim heard the crack of a whip and saw blood blossom on Merrill's cheek. Everyone's attention fell on the bald man with the whip. A man with a dark beard and a crooked grin that matched his crooked nose.

Merrill touched his hand to his cheek. He studied the blood on his fingers and didn't move.

Spoon placed a protective hand on Tim's shoulder.

The captain commanded, "Mr. Boggs, we have some new crewmen on board. Show them what happens when they don't follow orders."

Merrill understood too late. "No! I'll—"

Boggs grabbed Merrill and with the help of other men, soon had him stripped to the waist and tied to the mainmast.

"Please, no! I have a family!"

The crack of the whip shattered the air. It was followed by another, and then another. Merrill's screams and sobs followed each lashing.

Tears streamed down Tim's face. Surely someone would step forward and stop this horror.

Boggs continued the whipping until blood flowed freely down Merrill's back and legs.

Tim scanned the crew. They stood silently. Most looked down at the deck.

Tim whispered, "Mercy." He moved to take a step, but Spoon squeezed his shoulder and held him back. Tim's body shook.

When it was over, Merrill's lifeless body sagged against the mast. Blood seeped down his back, between the planks, and into the hold.

Tim's legs trembled, but he remained standing.

Captain Claymore addressed the crew. "Some of you are new. As you can see, on the ocean, on this ship, I am the law. I am like the lion of Africa, like a shark of the ocean! Do not cross me or First Mate Boggs, ever. If you follow orders, you will have the honor of serving on my crew. Just ask anyone, I am the best captain on the seas! Even pirates and privateers know to stay away from me. And, so I've been told, some sailors believe that God himself has a hand in guiding us. For the *Rota Fortunae* has never even struggled with foul weather." He scanned the men's faces, looking for antagonism. "Now get to work, I have goods to deliver to America!"

Tim stood still, wondering what they would do with Merrill's body. There were no words of commemoration, or even sewing the body in a bag, as was the custom. They lifted him from the deck and threw him over to the ocean, like rubbish.

Spoon whispered in his ear, "They call Boggs 'the Scorpion.' His sting is deadly." He gave Tim's shoulder a reassuring squeeze. "Come with me and be glad to make yourself useful."

* * * *

Tim and Spoon sat on deck in the open air, peeling potatoes. "Are you going to save any potatoes for us?" asked Spoon. Tim looked at him, confused. Spoon motioned to Tim's hands. "The potatoes, you're peeling them down to nothing."

Tim looked at the sliver of potato in his hands. He hadn't been paying attention. He had been staring at the hatch, daydreaming about the heathen down below. Five days had passed since Tim had been discovered on board. He had kept quiet and made himself useful. And for five days he watched and listened to the men. Now he tried to brush aside his daydream and focused on his job.

Tim picked up another potato and watched Spoon's dark hands deftly peel. "Spoon, may I ask you a question?"

Spoon picked up another potato. "Yes."

"I heard the crew talking about the man in chains. Is his name Kala?"

"Kaula."

"Why is everyone afraid of him?"

Spoon paused then continued his task. He casually glanced around to see if anyone was near. "Don't be bothering yourself about him."

"Is he dangerous? Why is he on board?"

Spoon stopped and looked directly at Tim. "Stay away from him, understand? You're a good lad. Don't cause trouble."

"But what kind of name is Kaula?"

Spoon sighed and elbowed Tim to get back to work. After a moment he whispered, "Some think he comes from Far West, some think he comes from the East, like Egypt or India." He shook his head. "I don't know. I've been with Captain Claymore for four years, and Kaula has always been with him." He looked around again. "There are things about him that just shouldn't be said."

"But—"

"Peel your potatoes, do your job, and mind your own affairs. Do *not* give Boggs any excuse to whip you, or worse. You've seen what he'll do."

"But I'm just a boy."

Spoon peeled potatoes. "Boys can disappear just as easily as men."

* * * *

The men sat at the table in the main mess and talked while they ate. Tim stayed busy refilling their cups and plates. "I say we're halfway to America. How long has it been, more than a month? We're halfway there."

"Aye! To America!" Campbell raised his cup for a toast.

"Campbell, you drink to anything."

"Aye!"

All the men laughed and toasted to America. This was Tim's favorite time of the day. The captain took his meals in his quarters with Boggs and Peters while, down in the galley, the men could be themselves. The camaraderie was evident. Most had signed on willingly, some had been crimped while drunk in taverns, some were indentured to masters in America, but after a month, all were now comrades at sea.

Bales, an experienced sailor, said, "Good swill here, Tim. You did this yourself?"

He stood tall. "Yes, sir."

"Spoon better keep an eye on you. You might have his job."

"No, thank you, sir. When I get to America, I plan to stay there."

Peters shouted from the deck, "Time to work, lads! Quit your yammering, there's work to be done! Spoon, Cap'n wants to see you!"

The men stood and scrambled to grab a few last bites of biscuit. Some gave Tim a pat on the back as they passed.

Spoon filled a bowl and placed a biscuit on top.

Tim knew this was for Kaula. "I can take his food to him."

Peters yelled from above, "Spoon!"

Spoon hesitated. "No, I'll do it. I don't want you near him." He hurried up the steps.

Tim stared at the simple meal. *How dangerous can he be? He's in chains.* Tim scooped up the bowl and went topside. He wondered if anyone would stop him. No one even glanced his way so he opened the hatch and descended into the dark. He was greeted with the clanking of chains.

There stood Kaula, just as he had seen him over a month ago. Tim knew Spoon kept him fed, but how did Kaula stay so big? Tim didn't know how to approach him. "Do I put this somewhere or do I hand it to you?"

Kaula stepped forward and Tim almost dropped the bowl. Kaula lifted his hands to accept it and Tim gave it to him. He was close enough now to see the chains were pinned to the floor and side of the ship. He turned to go.

"Thank you."

Tim turned around. "You're welcome." They studied each other. Tim was bursting with questions, but didn't know where to start, even if he dared. Kaula nodded. Tim felt as if he had been acknowledged and dismissed by a king. He walked up the steps thinking, *how is it a man in chains can seem more regal than a captain of a ship?*

* * * *

No matter what he tried, Tim could not fall asleep. He recalled Spoon's words when he returned from the Captain's quarters. "Where's the bowl?" He turned to Tim. "You took it to him."

"Yes, I gave him his food and talked to him. What harm can he do? He's chained to the ship."

Spoon studied Tim. "Sometimes things happen to people who've been around him."

"Silly superstition."

Spoon shook his head. "I believe there's more to it, but if I told you what I know, what I believe, you would think me mad."

"Tell me."

Spoon stared at Tim then said, "No, just stay away from him."

Tim couldn't get comfortable in his hammock. The bright moon seemed more like the sun, beckoning to him. His restlessness took over and he swung out and landed quietly. He took the lantern and told himself he was just getting some fresh air, but he knew he was lying. It was bright on deck, but dark in the hold.

He made his way across to the hatch. There was no guard nearby. He opened the hatch and went in. He lifted the lantern to peer into the darkness. Kaula's green eyes shone back. He sat calmly, as if expecting Tim.

In for a penny, in for a pound. "I'm sorry to bother you. I just wanted to ask you some questions."

Kaula motioned him to come closer.

The hair on the back of Tim's neck rose. He stopped just short of where he had given Kaula his food. "Why are you here? Why are you in chains? Did you do something bad?"

Kaula smiled. "It's been some time since I talked to a child."

"I'm not a child!"

Kaula put his hands up and motioned for Tim to calm down. "Sit down and I will tell you my story. I come from some islands far away."

"Like India?"

"If you went to India, you would only be halfway to my home."

Tim's eyes grew wide.

Kaula smiled and continued. "When I was younger, I wanted to go into the world and have adventures! I'm big, so it was easy to get jobs on the big ships. And people liked me, I'm a good worker. And then the thing happened." He slowly shook his head. "I was in port, drinking, laughing, having a merry time when a friend said, 'let us get tattoos!' Yes! Why not?"

Tim scooted closer.

"We walked and walked and found a place. It was a place with an old man who had tattoos all over, even on his face. I remember it was strange that he did not move like an old man and his eyes had a fire in them, intense.

"The man said, 'Would you like something no one else has?' Of course I did, I was young! Young men want to be like no one else.

"He reached up to a shelf and took down a very old book. He turned the pages and found a picture of a ship's wheel.

"'Perfect,' I said. He burned a strange plant and began to sing strange words and then I fell asleep. I awoke to someone shaking me. I was in the shop, but the man was gone. Everything in the shop was gone, no inks, no man, no book. The man who woke me was a stranger. He spoke to me in a language I did not know.

"And then the pain. My back was on fire, my shoulders, my neck! I cried out, 'What did he do to me?' The stranger spoke softly and took my hand. This tiny little man understood and led me, like I was a child, through the streets. I saw people and heard whispers. I knew I must look like a monster. I followed the man because I did not know what else to do."

Tim hugged himself and shivered.

"He led me into a little shop, a healer's shop. She mixed powders and oils and made a paste and put it on my back, and covered it with wet cloth strips. Oh, the relief! I was very grateful. She and the man argued. I could tell she did not want me there. After a time, they showed me with mirrors what I had become. They said things to me I did not understand. The man gave me a shirt to cover myself.

"I thanked them. I offered them the one coin I had left, but they refused. I thanked them many, many times. I needed to look for my ship, but did not know where to begin. The old man called out to a young boy. He told him something and the boy took my hand. Once again I was led through the streets. The boy led me to my ship. I thanked him and gave him my coin.

"My shipmates were happy to see me. They said, 'Where have you been? Was she worth it? It's been two days! We almost left without you!' I could not believe it, two days! I looked for my friend who had been with me, but he was not on the ship. Everyone thought he left for his home. I think the tattoo man did something to him. I know he did something to me."

Tim tried not to stare at the tattoo of the tentacle that crept up Kaula's neck.

"So now you want to know what I wanted to know on that first morning. What did the man do to me? Do you want to see?"

"Only if you want me to."

"It's fine." Kaula held up his finger. "But do not touch."

Kaula stood. He turned around and removed his shirt. Tim lifted the lantern and was amazed at what he saw. A tattoo of a ship's wheel covered Kaula's broad back. Inside each section of the wheel was a symbol. There was even a smaller wheel within the larger wheel, and it too had a symbol in each section. The four points of a compass were on the outside edges. The largest was the 'N' at the top marked with a scarlet chevron. There were also ocean scenes: a sea monster crushing a ship; a whaler, with harpoon ready, pursuing a wild-eyed sperm whale; and up on the right shoulder was a Kraken, its long tentacle reaching over and touching Kaula's throat. It was a magnificent piece of art.

Tim looked again at the whale. Its eye seemed to be looking at him. Tim could almost feel the poor animal's terror. He thought he saw the waves move. He blinked, then whispered, "What does it all mean?"

Kaula put on his shirt and turned around. "I do not know. I think only the man who did this knows."

"I think a few of the symbols are Egyptian, like some I saw this year at the new museum in London, but I have no idea what they mean. I recognize some animals, like a lion, and a crab." Tim proudly added, "I know those are constellations."

Kaula finished tying his shirt. Telling his story seemed to have tired him. "That is enough for tonight."

"But wait!" Tim raised his lantern. "Why does the captain keep you in chains?"

"Go on now, and listen to Spoon, he's a good man." Kaula sat down. Once again, Tim had been dismissed.

* * * *

Tim lurched up the steps from the galley, carrying a bucket in each hand. The choppy waters made it difficult as he fought for balance with each step, but a month ago he would have only been able to carry one bucket at a time. He paused and assessed the weight on each arm and liked how it felt. He thought about how much he had changed and wondered what his parents would think if they saw him now. He felt a twinge of regret that he hadn't had time to leave them a note. *The moment we land, I'll send a note home on the next ship to London. Maybe they'll be so glad I'm alive, they'll let me stay in Charleston.* He smiled, continued up to the deck and threw the scraps over the side. He turned and watched the crew.

Peters, standing nearby said, "Morning, Tim. All's well?"

"Yes, thank you." Over the last month Tim had gotten to know the crew. Tim thought Peters wasn't as bad as the captain or Boggs, but he seemed to be stuck between them and the crew.

Peters barked orders at the men. "Come on, ladies! Step lively!" The men, focused on their work, scrambled like mice over bags of grain. A shout from the bow chilled Tim's blood. It was Boggs.

"Oi! Watch yourself! You think you can knock me down? Do you think I don't know what you're about?" He raised his voice. "What you're all about? Mutiny, is what this is!" He grabbed Tom Green by the shirt. "I'll have to teach you a lesson!"

Green pleaded, "No! No, sir! It was the waves, sir! It was the waves. They made me bump into you!"

"I don't think so."

"Please, sir!"

The captain called down from the quarterdeck, "Boggs! What is it?"

"Nothing short of mutiny, sir!"

"No!" exclaimed Green.

"Mutiny? We don't have time for such nonsense! Deal with it!"

The men grumbled. Some began explaining.

"It were just an accident!"

"It was the waves, sir. The waves made him bump into Boggs."

"Green don't mean no harm, sir!"

Peters chimed in, "Green's a good man, sir."

Claymore stood with his arms crossed, legs wide apart. He looked down at the men and then out over the ocean.

The men resumed their work. Boggs seemed disappointed.

Then Claymore inquired, "Mr. Boggs, how shall we resolve this conflict?"

The men stopped and looked at each other. They liked Green, but didn't dare anger the captain or Boggs.

Tim was frozen to his spot. He wanted to stay on deck out of curiosity, but was afraid to draw attention to himself.

Captain Claymore raised a hand as if directing a ceremony. "Let the wheel decide!"

Some of the crewmen gasped and crossed themselves.

Mr. Bales spoke up. "No need for that, Captain. There's no problem here."

"I believe there is a problem, Mr. Bales. It's decided." The newer crew members watched the others with questioning looks. "Mr. Boggs, retrieve him."

Boggs smiled, let go of Green, and headed to the hold. He descended the steps and disappeared.

A few of the men pleaded. "No, Captain! Please, no!" They became silent and all eyes were on the hatch as they heard the clanking climb up the steps. Kaula emerged into the sunlight, both wrists and ankles bound. He squinted from the bright sun.

Boggs poked the back of his legs with his long knife. "Get a move on!"

"Easy now, Mr. Boggs," warned the captain.

Kaula stood there, eyes closed, as he took in the fresh salty air. He opened his eyes and appraised the crew. None of the men would look at him. His eyes found Tim and he let out a sigh.

"I said move!" Boggs poked him again.

Kaula shuffled across the deck to Claymore, who was now standing on the main deck. Kaula said, "Hello, John."

"It's 'Captain Claymore' while you're on my ship!"

Kaula stood in silence.

The captain smiled. "You men are going to see something you will never forget!"

Tim's fingers turned white from squeezing the ropes on the buckets.

The captain pulled a large key from his vest pocket and held it up to Kaula. "No problems from you. Hold out your hands." He unlocked the chains and sprang back.

Kaula massaged his wrists.

The captain ordered, "And now your shirt."

Kaula hesitated, then untied his shirt and removed it.

Some of the crew gasped. Tattoos were common among sailors, but they had never seen anything like his. Tim noted the colors were much more vivid in the sunlight.

Claymore nodded to Boggs and said, "Rope."

Boggs had the rope ready. Within minutes he had Kaula's wrists bound above his head and fastened to the mast. Boggs moved aside and stood next to Green.

Forgetting his fear, Tim took a step closer.

The captain paraded in front of Kaula, whose head hung in defeat. His long locks covered his face. The captain turned to the crew. "On this ship we have an exceptional way to answer questions." With a flourish of his hands he presented Kaula's back, like a magician in a show. He placed the palm of his hand on the tattoo and said, "And now you will see why I've named my ship the *Rota Fortunae,* which means 'wheel of fate!' O great Wheel of Fate, tell us what should we do? Does Mr. Green live… or die?" He stepped back and sneered at the crew.

The air grew heavy and Tim felt static prickle his skin. He watched the crew and they felt it too. The sun dimmed behind clouds. Tim thought a storm was approaching, but the waves became still. He looked out and the water around the ship was smooth while the waves farther away were choppy. *How is that possible?*

Spoon had come up from the galley and now approached him. "Come on down, Tim. You don't need to be near this."

Tim watched Kaula and whispered, "I think I do." Spoon stayed by his side.

The captain looked around and bared his teeth in a smile.

Kaula's hands grabbed the ropes and the muscles in his arms bulged, bracing for what was to come.

The air crackled with static. It grew louder and blue fingers of electricity danced across the deck and crew. Tim watched it run up the masts and play along the lines. It gravitated toward Kaula and, in a flash, it entered him. Kaula stiffened and his skin began to glow blue. The light grew brighter. He trembled and quaked. He threw his head back and let out a primal roar.

Every hair on Tim's body stood on end.

The glow faded and Kaula stopped shaking. His head hung down, limp. Then the tattoo came alive. The waves on his back flowed. The whaler, armed with a harpoon, moved back and forth, trying to gauge a perfect throw at the whale. The whale's tail pumped up and down, but didn't move forward. Its wild eye rolled around, looking for an escape that would never come. The Kraken's tentacles explored Kaula's neck and disappeared under his hair.

Tim and the crew gasped. Some of the men fell to their knees in prayer. Boggs smiled, poised and ready with knife in hand, beside Green.

The captain approached the tattoo again and asked, "O great Wheel of Fate, what is to become of Mr. Green? Let your compass guide us." He reached up and with a flick of his finger, he spun the wheels.

Tim whispered, "How can this be happening?"

The wheels slowed and then stopped. The symbol in the outer wheel, below the North chevron, was a green tree. The symbol chosen from the inner wheel looked similar to a cross.

Mr. Bales declared, "He lives! Surely the green tree means life. Mr. Green lives!"

"Aye!" said Campbell. "And that there is an Egyptian cross. I've seen 'em when I sailed north o' Africa."

The captain stared at the wheels and then he faced the crew. "Don't you see? It clearly means that Mr. Green is the tree and the cross represents God. Mr. Boggs, send him off!"

Boggs, quick as a snake, stepped behind Green and slit his throat. Blood sprayed in an arc and Green collapsed on the deck.

The men cried out in dismay. Boggs held up the bloody knife, ready for any reprisal.

The crew stood in shock. They watched Green grab at his throat, trying to staunch the blood that sprayed through his fingers and onto the deck. Bales rushed to his side. He took off his shirt and pressed it against the wound. Green looked at Bales, grasped his arm, and gurgled. A minute later he was dead.

Bales moaned, "No, no, no, no." He gently closed Green's eyes then clenched both of his fists. He rose and faced Boggs.

Boggs smiled.

Bales turned to the captain. "Captain! I've served with you for some years now and neither you nor Mr. Boggs has ever gone against the wheel. Now I don't like the thing, it scares the devil out of me, but it has always had a kind of logic to its answers and we have always followed them."

Boggs sneered. "You want to be next?"

The captain said, "Down, Mr. Boggs. Mr. Bales has always been a valuable member of this crew, even though he is replaceable. You have enough to do with Mr. Green and Kaula. Peters, help Mr. Boggs take him down before Kaula wakes. And clean this mess off my ship."

The sky cleared and the ship resumed its normal rocking. But Tim knew nothing would ever be normal again.

* * * *

That night Tim volunteered to take Kaula's food to him. Spoon asked, "You still want to go into the hold with him, after what you saw today?"

Tim nodded. "I want him to explain what happened."

Spoon handed him the bowl. "Good luck. He's never talked to any-one about it."

Tim stopped at the door and turned around. "Spoon, does the wheel ever pick something good?"

"Yes, once we argued about which course to sail. Some said we should go north around a storm. It was a faster route, but dangerous. Others said we should take the safer route to the south. We spun the wheel and it told us to go south. We went south."

"How do you know it was the right decision?"

"A fleet of ships were in the north and were caught in the storm. All were lost. I think the wheel knew and saved us."

"What is it?"

Spoon shook his head. "I have no idea. Some men think it's from the devil, some think it's God's instrument."

"What do you think?"

"I think the wheel wants to survive."

"Why is that?"

"I've been watching and I think it doesn't allow any mortal harm come to Kaula. He's a nice enough fellow, but death surrounds him. I believe that at least three men have died because of it. Bigelow fell overboard and was taken by a shark before we could reach him, Hudson caught a fever and died, and Davidson was struck by lightning. Later I learned that Bigelow and Hudson hated and feared Kaula so much that they planned to kill him. I don't know about Davidson, maybe it was chance that lightning struck him. But I do know that he and Kaula had an argument and the next day, out of a clear blue sky, lightning struck him. After that, no one will talk to Kaula or go near him."

"Do the other men think the same?"

"We don't talk about it, but I think so."

"I don't think anything will happen to me." Tim picked up the bowl and grabbed a lantern. He walked to the hatch and stared at it, as if trying to see what was on the other side. He was afraid, terrified, but he had to know more about the blue light and the wheel.

One of the crew, a man named Tanner, asked him, "You ain't afraid?"

Tim was so lost in his own thoughts, Tanner's voice sounded far away. Tanner shrugged, then opened the hatch for him.

There's nothing for it. I have to know. He walked down the steps. The lamplight illuminated Kaula, standing in his chains.

Tim placed the bowl on a barrel and held up the lamp to study him.

Kaula didn't move. "So what do you think of me now, young Tim? You must be very brave to come see me. Spoon is the only person who will come down and even he won't speak."

Tim mustered his courage. "I have to know what happened. Is it you? Do you control it?"

Kaula closed his eyes and shook his head. "No, I have no control over this… evil thing."

"How did you come to be on this ship, in these circumstances?"

Kaula picked up his bowl and sat heavily on the floor. He took a bite of food and then continued with his story.

"I told you how I awoke to find this monster of a thing on me. It healed. I never removed my shirt. I tried to hide it until one day, many weeks later after a long heat spell, it rained. Everyone was happy and dancing in the rain. I forgot about it and removed my shirt.

"I got many stares and then some of the men laughed. They said I must have been really drunk. How could I tell them the truth? So I smiled and agreed. What else could I do? I was glad it was not a secret anymore. We went back to work.

"But the men talked about me and one man said he didn't like it. He said it looked like dark magic, and since I came from unchristian islands, maybe I was dark magic too. I faced him. He had a cruel smile. I could tell he was going to cause me trouble.

"He was a man who liked to hear himself talk and soon all the men stopped work to hear him. He had them grab me and turn me around. He was mocking me and when he touched my back, I got a bad feeling, like an itching on my skin."

Tim thought he knew exactly what he meant. He wondered if it was like the static he had felt.

"He liked the attention and said, 'Wheel, show us what you do.'

"I heard the crackle and saw the blue light. I thought the storm has returned but then I felt like my whole body was on fire. I thought I was dying, and then all went black. When I awoke, I was in a dinghy with a crewmate rowing. He told me what happened. He told me about the blue light, and how the wheel spinned and the tattoo moved. Lightning struck the big talker and killed him. The men wanted to kill me, but the man in the rowboat saved me. He convinced them to give us a boat and set us adrift. I thanked him and told him I was in his debt forever."

"I'm glad he was there to save you."

Kaula finished the food. He placed the bowl on the barrel. "I wish they had killed me. That man was John Claymore."

Tim whispered, "Captain Claymore."

"Yes."

"Begging your pardon, but you're so much bigger than he. How is it that you're here in chains?"

"He tricked me. He told me I'd be his first mate and we'd make a fortune in shipping. Just before we left on our first voyage, he told me to check the cargo and Boggs and Peters and another man were waiting down here with the chains. I fought, but I've been down here ever since."

"But why?"

"Because he thinks it keeps me safe. As long as I'm on board, nothing will happen to the ship. I remember he said, 'We will be the most celebrated and trustworthy vessel in all of Britain.'"

Tim pondered that a moment, then asked, "Kaula, how many years have you been down here?"

Kaula squeezed his eyes shut and gritted his teeth. Tears streamed down his face. This surprised Tim that a man of his size and demeanor would cry.

Kaula raised his manacled wrists, palms up in defeat. "For eternity."

On impulse Tim said, "I'll free you. I don't know how, but I'll free you."

"No, Tim, you must not. Do not try."

"Who would suspect me? I can get the key." As soon as he said the words, his skin crawled at the thought.

"No. What good would it do, out here in the middle of the ocean?"

"But I have to help you!"

"Let me think on this."

And just as before, Tim was dismissed. He took the bowl but left the lantern. It wasn't much, but at least he could give Kaula some light.

* * * *

Tim rushed around the table, trying to keep the men's bowls and cups filled.

Bales asked, "Is Spoon feeling any better?"

Tim was too busy to even look at him. "No, sir. His fever just seems to get worse."

"Well, I'm grateful that your cooking has improved. I'm sure the other men are too."

"Aye!" exclaimed Campbell. The other men laughed and concurred.

Tim couldn't help but smile. It felt good to be appreciated and to feel a part of the crew. He had proven himself to be a hard worker and a decent cook. It was no surprise to Tim that when the food was good, the men were happier.

After he filled the bowls, Bales drew him aside. "So Spoon's no better?"

"He's worse. The surgeon has never seen the likes of it."

Bales stroked his chin. "It's been two weeks. Surely if it were catching, one of us would have it by now."

Tim shrugged. "I don't know, sir."

Campbell joined them when Bales asked Tim, "Do you recall when it struck him?"

That was easy for Tim to recall. He remembered the night that Kaula had told him about Claymore. Tim returned to fo'c'sle, eager to share the story with Spoon. When he approached him, Spoon was delirious with fever. Tim whispered to Bales, "It's been two weeks. It struck the night right after Mr. Green."

Bales sighed and nodded. Tim wondered if Mr. Bales was thinking the same thing he was, that Spoon's illness was connected to the wheel. Was it because Spoon talked to Kaula? Did the wheel see Spoon as a threat?

Campbell chimed in. "It's that heathen. You haven't talked to him too, have you, boy?"

"Yes."

Campbell and Bales looked at each other and then at Tim. Bales patted Tim on the back. "Good meal, son."

"Thank you, sir."

Bales said to the men, "Let's get back to work! We still have an ocean to cross and you lot aren't getting any prettier. I don't know about you, but I'm ready to set my feet on land!"

The men chuckled and headed up the steps.

Campbell patted Tim on the back. "Good meal." He gave Tim a weak smile and he looked like he wanted to say something else, but turned to leave. As he approached the steps he wiped his eyes and muttered, "Damn sea salt, makes me eyes water."

* * * *

The next morning Tim awoke to the bellowing of the captain on deck. "Spoon! Spoon! Get up here!"

Tim wiped the sleep from his eyes and checked on Spoon. He was still the same, unconscious and feverish.

A handful of men entered the fo'c'sle. Campbell said, "Cap'n wants to see Spoon."

"But he's still ill."

The men clustered around the hammock. "But the Cap'n wants to see him. I'm sorry, but what choice do we have? We wish it weren't like this. But we do as we're told, or it's Boggs for us." The men grabbed Spoon against Tim's protests. They carried him up to the captain as Tim followed.

The captain ordered, "Bring him to me." The men laid him at the captain's feet. He poked Spoon with his foot. "Get up, Spoon. Enough is enough. I've given you plenty of time to recuperate."

Spoon didn't move.

Tim stepped forward. "He's sick, Captain."

"Not too sick to work."

"It's fine, sir. He can rest. I'll continue to do the cooking."

The captain studied Tim. "Then I suppose if we don't need him anymore, we should throw him overboard."

Bales stepped forward. "Begging your pardon, Captain. He's no trouble."

Claymore's mouth pursed. "He is most assuredly causing trouble! Are you arguing with me?"

"No, sir…"

"Mr. Boggs!" Boggs appeared by his side just like the lap dog he was. "Mr. Boggs, fetch the wheel."

Tim groaned, "Oh, Lord." He knelt by Spoon and cradled him. "Wake up, Spoon. Wake up!"

The men milled around and muttered amongst themselves. Soon Boggs appeared with Kaula.

The captain never seemed happier than when he had the chance to torment Kaula. "It seems we have a stalemate as to old Spoon's fate. He's probably just as good as dead anyway. We'll let the wheel decide if we should throw him overboard."

Tim looked up at Kaula, searching for help.

Boggs poked Kaula with his long knife. "C'mon, you know what to do."

Kaula refused to move forward and Boggs slashed at his thigh.

"Steady there, Mr. Boggs!"

Blood seeped through the fabric as Kaula moved to the mast. Boggs removed the chains and fastened the ropes to Kaula's wrists.

Tears streamed down Tim's face and he shook Spoon. "Wake up! Wake up!"

Captain Claymore paraded in front of the wheel. "O great and wise wheel. What shall we do with old Spoon? Should we throw him to the sharks or let him go back to his soft hammock?"

Once again the air crackled with static and blue electricity played along the ship's lines. It ran across the deck, found Kaula, and flew into him. He stiffened, glowed blue, and then shook uncontrollably. The shaking stopped and the glow faded. His chin dropped to his chest and the tattoo moved.

It was just as Tim remembered it. The whalers in their boat pursued the whale whose eye searched for an escape.

"What is Spoon's fate?" The captain reached up and spun the wheel. Everyone grew quiet and stepped closer.

Tanner whispered to Campbell, "What is it? I can't see."

Campbell answered, "I don't know what it means. It's a lion and a scorpion."

Claymore announced, "A lion! Sharks are the lions of the sea. Throw him to the sharks!"

Tim's mind raced frantically for an escape and he seized upon an idea. He stood and shouted, "No!"

The crew gasped.

The captain sneered. "We must do as the wheel says."

Tim walked up to the captain and stood four feet in front of him, legs apart, and tried to be as intimidating as he could be. "That is what you always do? You do what the wheel says?"

Claymore laughed as if the child amused him. "Of course." He turned to the men, expecting support. They looked at him in silence. His smile wavered.

Tim challenged, "I think the wheel means you, Captain, you and Mr. Boggs. More than once you've called yourself the lion of the sea and Mr. Boggs is called The Scorpion. I think the wheel has chosen *you*!" He was full of fire and couldn't stop. He pointed at the captain. "And I also think that you were supposed to let Mr. Green live! That is why Spoon is sick. He got sick the night after you and Boggs murdered Mr. Green! Spoon is paying for your mistake!"

Claymore's face blossomed red. Boggs sheathed his knife and removed the whip from his belt. "Should I teach him a lesson, Cap'n?"

Tim's entire body shook, but he stood his ground. "It is you, Captain! The wheel has chosen you!"

Claymore roared, "Kill him! Kill the boy and that stupid lazy cook! Make them pay! I want this boy's blood to wash across my deck!"

Boggs raised the whip and with a flick of his wrist there was a crack like a gunshot. Tim felt the sting on his neck, then the growing fire from the cut. He felt the blood trickle down his neck. He watched Boggs lift his arm again and Tim raised his own to protect himself. His mind flashed back to Merrill's death. He wanted to run, his mind raced to think of a hiding place, but he knew it was hopeless. There was no place to hide on a ship. He fell to his knees then heard a roar deeper and more primal than the captain's. He expected the sting of fire from the next lash of the whip, but it didn't come. He peeked through his arms and saw Kaula standing and facing them. Kaula was awake and his left hand was free. It was dark red with blood that flowed down from the wrist to the fingertips and dribbled onto the deck. His right wrist was still bound, but the rope was free from the mast and pooled around his feet.

The captain screeched, "Mr. Boggs, Peters, secure him!"

Boggs faced Kaula. They bellowed and ran at each other, colliding like sparring bulls. They fell to the deck and rolled around, punching, and grasping for the best hold.

Tim felt the vibrations of each blow travel through the deck, up his legs, and into his stomach. He stood in awe of the size, strength, and ferocity of the men.

This spurred the crew to retaliate. Peters jumped out of the way as the men grabbed what they could use as weapons. They pulled Boggs from Kaula. Years of anger spilled out and were unleashed upon Boggs.

Tim was still too stunned to move. The men who had been his friends were now wild and uncontrollable beasts. Tim ran to Spoon and pulled him aside to safety. Kaula was on his hands and knees, gasping for air.

Boggs fought back, but it was useless. He dragged himself to the edge of the ship, leaving a bloody trail. The crew watched as he pulled himself up. He pointed at them and said, "You sorry sons o' whores, you think you can kill me? Come on! Come on!"

The men ran at him again. They hacked and chopped. Within seconds he was dead and, without any guilt or remorse, they threw him overboard.

"Nooooo!" screamed the captain, staring at the spot where Boggs went over.

The men looked at Peters, who held up his hands in surrender.

Kaula rose to his feet. "It's over, John."

Claymore clenched his fists. "You've never been good luck. You're a curse! I regret the moment I saved you!"

"So do I, but I'll never go down below again. I would rather die."

"So be it." The captain pulled out his knife and charged.

Kaula readied himself. He met the attack by grabbing the captain's right wrist with his bloody hand and pummeled Claymore with his right. Captain Claymore took blow after blow while landing a few of his own.

The crew cheered on Kaula.

"Watch that knife!"

"Captain's got a hard head!"

"Mind the rope!"

The two enemies struggled on the deck, crashing against crates and equipment. Kaula fought with a pent up vengeance while trying to keep the fight away from Spoon and Tim. He pinned down the captain. Claymore slipped his hand free and slashed Kaula's chest.

Kaula slapped the knife from Claymore's grip. It clattered and skidded across the wooden deck.

The captain squirmed around and got enough room to roll over and crawl away, but Kaula grabbed his feet and pulled him back. Claymore grasped around. His hand landed on the rope that led to Kaula's right wrist. He grabbed it, kicked free of Kaula's grasp, turned over and launched himself against Kaula's chest for a last attack.

Kaula fell backward, his arms behind him to break his fall. He landed in a gap between stacked crates and was wedged between them, his arms trapped behind him.

The captain sat on Kaula's chest and cackled as he wrapped the rope around Kaula's neck. "I want you to die and go to the devil that made you."

Kaula wriggled like a fish on a hook.

Tim cried out, "Someone help him!"

Mr. Bales stepped forward but Peters put out an arm to hold him back.

Tim laid Spoon on the deck and stood up.

The captain pulled tighter on the rope. Suddenly he screamed, "No! No! God, no!"

The crew couldn't see what was happening. The sounds of Claymore's screams were so horrible, the crew rushed to the opposite side of the ship. Tim ran to Kaula. The captain's screams had turned to gasps and choking. Kaula's arms were still pinned behind him and his eyes were wide with horror. Tim looked at the captain to see what Kaula saw.

The Kraken's dark tentacles trailed from Kaula's neck, up the captain's arms, and covered his neck and face. Tim stood transfixed, watching the captain's skin move and tighten. Claymore's lips turned blue and he became still. The tentacles withdrew and returned to Kaula's shoulder.

Tim pulled the Captain's lifeless body off Kaula. Kaula was visibly shaken, but steadied himself. He looked down at Claymore's contorted face. Kaula picked him up, and threw him into the sea.

The men slowly returned to the middle of the ship. Tim retrieved the captain's knife and cut the rope from Kaula's wrist. Tim wondered if the crew knew what really happened. *Better to let them think he did it with his own hands than the truth.*

An uneasy silence filled the air.

Finally Campbell asked, "What do we do now? Who's to be captain?"

Tim asked Kaula, "How about you?"

"No. As soon as we dock, I'm staying on land. I've had enough of ships." He looked at the men who couldn't return his gaze, except Mr. Bales. "I think Mr. Bales would make a good captain."

The men brightened at the idea and patted Mr. Bales on the back. Even Peters seemed to agree.

Mr. Bales nodded. "I'll do my best."

Tanner asked, "What'll we tell people when we reach port? We could hang for what we done."

Campbell offered, "A storm carried them overboard?"

Mr. Bales shook his head. "No, let's say they killed each other. Both were known for their tempers. It's believable."

Spoon moaned.

Tim exclaimed, "Spoon!" and rushed to his side. He cradled Spoon in his arms. The crew gathered around them.

Without opening his eyes, Spoon whispered, "I'm so thirsty. Am I on deck? How did I get here?"

Tim smiled and said, "We have a long story to tell you."

MOME RATH, MY SWEET

GALE ALBRIGHT

Joey Dormouse was dead and I was heading for a fall.

I hunkered in a filthy downtown alley, backed against a slimy brick wall, sweating under my fedora. It looked like my number was up this time. I had gone through the war without a scratch, dodging Kraut bullets at the Battle of the Bulge. Was I going to die in post-war Hollywood, shot by a trigger-happy cop for a crime I didn't commit? My mug was plastered on the front page of all the newspapers, right under the headline: "Private Eye Wanted for Murder."

All because somebody shot Joey Dormouse. I was innocent but who would believe a low-rent private dick? This was a dirty town, full of dirty people with dirty minds. I was being set up. If the cops didn't shoot me, I'd go to the gas chamber.

I thought back to the dame. If only I hadn't taken this case. If only I had given the dame her walking papers. If only I hadn't got lost in those big green eyes. But when I saw her shapely form at my office door, I let her walk right in. I remember it like it was yesterday, because it was yesterday.

I was sitting in my dingy office, waiting for the phone to ring. And waiting and waiting. I finally called my answering service.

"Grimm Investigations," said the tired, female voice.

"Put some enthusiasm into it. I don't run a morgue. Got any calls for me? Any new clients?"

The voice went from tired to sour. "Oh, it's you, Mr. Grimm. Nope, nothing. Nobody's called. My boss, Chick Little, has a bone to pick with you about your account. Looks like you're overdue to the tune of—"

I hung up. Chick Little's answering service was for the birds. I had paid my account in full a few months ago when I was flush from a case, but I guess more time had passed than I thought. Chick was always clucking about not getting his greenbacks on time.

I had decided to go downstairs to Harley's Barbershop for a shave when there was a knock on my office door. My office only had one room.

I wasn't one of those high-toned private dicks with a peroxide-blonde secretary in the front office with a typewriter and a steno pad. I was strictly a one-horse operation.

I straightened up in my swivel chair. I could see what looked like a female form—and I mean female—through the frosted top half of my door. The one that had my name stenciled on it.

"Come in," I said.

The door opened.

A dame stepped into my office.

When I say a dame, it's like calling a Reo a jalopy or the Empire State Building a shack. You get my drift.

Speaking of drift, the dame drifted into my office, turned up her beautiful puss at my shabby quarters, and calmly opened her purse. She pulled out a wad of greenbacks.

"Do you think this will be enough?" she asked, focusing her emerald green eyes in my direction. She wore one of those big picture hats like Scarlett O'Hara. Scarlet hair curled around her shoulders.

You had to be slick with high-toned dolls like this. I slithered out of my swivel chair and leaned on my desk. I lit a Lucky Strike, taking my own sweet time about it. I inhaled, then fixed her with my baby blues.

"Enough for what, girlie?"

"Enough for you to find my sister?"

I reached out and swiped the dough from her hand. I counted it. Well, well, it was over three hundred dollars. I'd hit the big time, for sure. But I didn't let on.

"That'll do—for now," I said, stuffing the bankroll in my inside suit pocket. "What's your sister's name and how much trouble is she in?"

She sat down in my visitor's chair and crossed her shapely legs. I got my mind out of the gutter and got down to business.

"Well, speak up, sister. I haven't got all day." I did have all day, as a matter of fact, but it was bad for business to admit things like that. I wondered what a high-rent lady like this was doing in my low-rent office. Maybe she used the phone book to find me. But "Grimm Investigations" was pretty far down in the alphabet. She looked like she could afford one of those classy private agencies with secretaries and carpets. Maybe she was into something illegal.

"My name is… well, you can call me Miss Wonderland," she said, taking a cigarette out of a gold case. I leaned forward and gave her a light.

She took a delicate puff. "I don't want any attention from the police. Find my sister and let me know where she is. That's all you have to do."

"What's your sister's name?"

"Alice. Alice Wonderland."

"When's the last time you saw her?"

"Three days ago. Monday afternoon. We were having cocktails at the Brown Derby. Our waiter said Alice had a telephone call and directed her to the office. She never came back. When I questioned the waiter, he said she took the call and went to the powder room. She just disappeared."

"Do you remember the waiter's name?"

"I think it was Johnny. No, it was Joey."

"Did you ask Joey who called her?"

"Yes, I did. He said it was a man, a Mister Rath. I have no idea who he is."

Was this dame kidding me?

"Mister Rath? Could it have been Mome Rath?"

"Why, yes, yes, that was his name. How did you—?"

"Come on lady, where have you been? Don't you read the papers?"

She frowned, in puzzlement, I thought, but she could have been trying to con me.

"Mome Rath is only the biggest gangster since Al Capone. He's the most notorious hood on the West Coast."

"My sister would never be involved with a person like that," she said. I wondered if she was playing me for a sucker.

"Alice is a sweet, innocent young woman," she continued. "In fact, she's lived most of her life in Baja California, in the convent of Santa Maria in Mucho Sur, not far from Tijuana."

"Do you have a picture of her?"

She fumbled through her expensive handbag. "Here. This one was taken not long ago."

I took the photograph from her hand. It was a picture of a sweet-looking young girl with long blond hair and big blue eyes. The blue the color of turquoise in a silver setting. Her hair the color of a golden palomino riding in the Old Western Days parade. You get my drift. What a beauty. So pure, so innocent, so…. Then I noticed she was standing with a bunch of nuns in black habits. Behind them was what looked like an old Spanish mission, with tropical flowers climbing up the walls.

"Where have you been all the time she was in this convent?"

"I'm quite a bit older than Alice. Our parents are dead, so I sent Alice to school at the convent when she was six years old. I went to work so I could support us. I wanted to make sure she was in a good place."

I looked at the "other" sisters in the photograph. The ones with black veils on their heads. "I guess that would be a good place for her," I said. "Where did you work, and doing what, may I ask?"

"I was a nightclub singer," she said. "In San Francisco. It was the only way I could earn enough money to take care of us. I saw her as much as I could, but it was hard getting away from work."

"No need to feel bad," I said. "You did your best to take care of your kid sister." I paced around the office, trying to think. "What was she doing in the Brown Derby on Monday afternoon? Did she run away from the convent?"

"Yes, yes, she did, Mr. Grimm. She ran away and called me to meet her in the Brown Derby. You can imagine how shocked I was. I tried to talk her into going back, but she said—"

I interrupted. "She said she was through with school. She wanted to come live with you in San Francisco. Am I right?"

She smiled at me. "Why, yes, you are a good detective. That's exactly it. She said she was tired of being in the convent and wanted to live with me."

"But what about the phone call from this Mome Rath character?" I said, stopping my pacing. "How would she ever meet a guy like that?"

She shook her head. "I have no idea. I was surprised when the waiter said she had a phone call. I didn't think she knew a soul in Hollywood. And then, she vanished."

She dabbed at her face with a dainty, lace-trimmed hanky. "Please, Mr. Grimm. Please find Alice for me. When I think of that poor, innocent girl...."

"Don't worry," I said, snapping on my fedora. "I'm going to find her. Where can I reach you?"

She bit her luscious red lips. "Don't try to reach me. I'll come back to your office day after tomorrow. You can give me a report then. I'm not going back home until Alice is with me."

"Try not to worry, Miss Wonderland. I know how to find missing persons."

She got up from the chair, put her gloves back on, and opened the office door. She turned her head to look at me, just once, then walked out. Her stocking seams were as straight as Mome Rath was crooked. What a looker.

I touched the bankroll in my pocket. It was time to go to the Brown Derby and make this waiter talk about the mysterious phone call from Mome Rath to a kid who'd spent most of her life in a convent in Baja California.

* * * *

It's not every day I get thrown out of the Brown Derby, but today was the day. I don't know what they were so upset about. I told them a dame was missing but they said it didn't excuse my slapping a waiter around. Well, that particular weasel, Joey Dormouse, deserved to be slapped on the hour, every hour. He denied everything. Said he never even saw Alice Wonderland or her gorgeous red-headed sister on Monday. Said he never heard of Mome Rath. I twisted his arm and gave him a sock in the puss to refresh his memory.

"You're permanently blackballed from this establishment!" shouted the head guy as he pitched me out the front door. "Try to come back and I'll call the police."

I picked myself off the pavement and found my fedora. It was slightly the worse for wear. He didn't have to step on it. Usually I'm the subtle kind of dick who gets his information with smooth calculation, but sometimes I get tired of people lying to me. And that waiter was lying to me. He tried to pretend there had never been a phone call for Alice Wonderland from Mome Rath.

I stopped at a park and lit a Lucky Strike. There was a cover-up going on. I could feel it. All over this murky, dark, deceitful, treacherous, diabolical town. Oh, it looked good to the tourists, all that glitter and glamour, but I knew about the sewer that ran underneath all the gold.

I flicked the dirt off my fedora, jammed it on my head, and marched down the street. I was looking for answers, and fast. Why had Joey Dormouse lied? Did Mome Rath have his tentacles into the Brown Derby? What did he want with Alice Wonderland?

I was thinking hard about everything when I opened my office door. I must have been thinking hard because I didn't notice the door was unlocked until I got inside. Then I felt a cold, hard, steel gat press against the back of my neck.

I slowly raised my hands. "Looks like you have the advantage of me," I said.

No answer.

"Mind if I turn around?"

The gat moved away from my neck. I was about to say something else when a mountain fell on my head. I fell all the way down the mountain and slid into a deep, black lake.

The lake turned into a long, dark tunnel. Down, down, down I went. As I went flying by I saw gin bottles and blondes, brunettes and whiskey bottles, all whirling around me. On and on I went, faster and faster. Suddenly, I hit bottom. My face kissed gritty, cold, stinking, damp concrete. I slowly picked myself up and looked around. My fedora was still on my head. I moved my arms and legs. Looked like no broken bones. I found my pack of Luckies and took out a smoke. When I struck a match, the darkness slipped away for a moment. It looked like I was in a cellar. I used the match to guide me to a set of stairs before it went out and burned my trigger finger.

Trigger? I felt for my gat. Whew, it was still in my shoulder holster. Whoever attacked me was a two-bit gunsel. Too dumb to pat me down for a weapon. But it was lucky for me. Now I could get the drop on him—or them. I was in the dark but I would find my way out of this dump.

I felt my way up the slimy stairs and opened a door at the top. Pulling my rod from its holster, I stuck my head out. There was a corridor, dark and dingy, with cheap light bulbs providing a minimum of light. A radio was blaring big band music from behind one of the doors. Loud voices were raised across the hall. Some floozy and a guy, it sounded like, haggling over money. I had spent a lot of time in dingy, dirty, low-light hotel corridors like this with my camera, looking to bust in on adulterous couples and take pictures for a quick divorce action. The private eye racket was as dirty as they come. Especially if you were the low-rent type, like me, Jake Grimm, Hollywood P.I.

I found the elevator at the end of the hall.

"Take me to the front desk," I told the operator. He was a wrinkled old guy wearing a striped suit with a cigarette stuck in his puss. The elevator was full of smoke. I coughed. "What's your name, pal?"

"Cheshire."

"Chester?"

"No, Cheshire."

Chester was drunk. Couldn't even pronounce his own name. He was a wet brain on his way to the laughing academy. No wonder he was running an elevator in a rat trap like this. When he pulled open the door, I stepped out into the lobby. I turned back to ask him a question, but the elevator door was closed. He had turned tail on me.

The clerk at the front desk was drumming his paws on the counter. He was as jumpy as a hophead who'd run out of dope.

"Hey, pal, what's the name of this establishment?" I asked, lighting a cigarette. I offered him one, but he shook his head so fast, his whiskers fluttered. The guy had white hair and white whiskers and a pale face. I bet he was an albino.

"What's your name, fella?"

"Whitey," he squeaked. That didn't surprise me. Of course it was.

"Well, Whitey, I asked you a question."

He gulped and pulled a pocket watch out of his vest. It was an old watch, solid gold from the looks of it. How did an albino working in a place like this own a solid gold pocket watch?

"Look, mister, it's getting late. I'm going to have to ask you to leave. I'm late for an appointment."

I reached forward and grabbed him by the lapels of his jacket. "What's the name of this flop house, Whitey? And make it snappy."

"The Queen Hotel. Now, please, I've got to go. I'm closing the office now."

The albino was trying to rabbit out on me. I felt like slapping his twitchy nose.

I grabbed him again.

"You're not going anywhere, pal, until I get the truth. Where's Alice Wonderland?"

Whitey twisted away from me and disappeared into a doorway behind the counter. I vaulted over and twisted the door knob, but it wouldn't budge. I banged on the door. No answer.

It was time to bring out the heavy artillery. I threw myself against the door, again and again. All I got was a sore shoulder.

Suddenly the door opened.

A dame stood in front of me.

When I say a dame, it was like calling a filet mignon a hamburger, or Veronica Lake Ma Kettle. You get my drift.

She drifted toward me. She had a willowy frame and big brown eyes. Her brown hair was braided on top of her shapely head. She wore a white blouse and a black skirt. She had a pencil stuck behind her ear.

"Can I help you, mister?" Her voice was melodious.

"Where's Whitey?" I asked. She might be a swell skirt, but I knew how to handle them.

"Oh, he has a very important appointment. I can help you. My name's Mary Ann. I work the night shift."

"What's a gal like you doing in a place like this?" I gestured at the threadbare lobby and dark shadows.

"I don't know what you mean," she said, smiling at me. "This is a fine hotel. It's very old. It has character."

Two could play this game. "Speaking of characters, doll, I need to ask your boss a question."

Mary Ann loosened her braided hair and fluffed it out around her shapely face. She took the pencil from behind her ear and doodled on a pad of paper on the counter. "Why don't you ask me, instead?"

I sighed. Whitey was probably a million miles away by now. Smart move, shoving a gorgeous broad in front of me.

"Okay. Where's Alice Wonderland?"

She smiled. "Do you think she's prettier than I am? Is that why you want to know?"

I slammed my fist down on the counter. "Quit playing me for a sap, lady. I'm a private dick. I've got a job to do, and that job is to find Alice Wonderland. Somebody kidnapped me and put me in your cellar. I'm tired of the runaround. Tell me the truth or I'll take you downtown and you can talk to the coppers."

"No need to get mean, friend," she said, her brown eyes all big and wounded. "I'll tell you where she is."

That was more like it. I squared my shoulders. I didn't like being mean to cute dolls, but enough was enough. I had a job to do. Even if she had big eyes and swirly hair and lots of red lipstick.

She reached into her purse and pulled out a piece of chocolate cake. "My mother makes my lunch every time I go to work. She makes the best chocolate cake in the world. Would you like a bite?"

"No, thanks. Where's Alice?"

Big, sad eyes again. "Oh, please, have a bite to show there's no hard feelings, okay, mister? Then I'll tell you everything you want to know. I promise."

Well, if it would stop her from making those puppy dog eyes at me, okay.

"One bite. One bite only. Then you give me the information, got it, sister?"

"Sure. Here, have a bite. You'll love it."

She had produced a silver fork from somewhere, and speared a piece of cake on the points. She held it up to my mouth.

"Open wide, now, that's a good boy." Her voice was melodious again.

I opened my mouth. She pushed the tip of the fork in, gently, and a moist, chocolaty, gooey chunk of cake rolled onto my tongue.

I chewed. It seemed to melt in my mouth. I kept on chewing. That's because she put another chunk in my mouth. I wanted to refuse it, but I couldn't stop. I ate the whole piece of cake.

"Well, you must have been hungry," she said. "What an appetite. You're like a little pink piggy."

Nobody called me a little pink piggy and got away with it. Nobody.

"I'm not a… a little…. I'm not a…. What did you say?"

My head was spinning around. I blinked my eyes a few times. I felt like I'd had three shots of bourbon. What was in that cake?

Somebody hit me on the head. I whirled around, reaching into my shoulder holster, but there was nobody behind me. My head had hit the ceiling. A dingy light fixture swung by my nose. I couldn't get my hands on my rod because my elbows kept banging into the walls of the lobby.

Down below me, way down, Mary Ann was staring up at me. She looked like she was a million miles away. I had turned into a giant!

"What was in that cake?"

"Eat this. Maybe it will help," she yelled. She sounded far away. She stood on top of one of my wingtips. "I'll toss it to you," she said.

Mary Ann cranked up her throwing arm and something flew up at me. I don't know how I managed to catch it. My elbows were jammed into the walls and I was too big to bend over, but I caught it in my open palm.

It was a tiny yellow thing.

"It's a piece of cheese," she yelled. "Eat it."

I didn't know why I should trust her, but what choice did I have?

I ate the tiny yellow speck. I guess it tasted like cheese, but it was smaller than a bread crumb. I swallowed. Nothing happened. I was about to shout at her again, when I got dizzy.

I felt like I was in an elevator, going from the penthouse all the way to the lobby, with no stops in between.

Splat! I hit the lobby floor. I felt to see if my nose was broken. I saw a pair of big, black, round things in front of me. Picking myself up, I reached out and touched one. It felt like leather. I looked up.

I was touching Mary Ann's shoes! Now she was the giant. She smiled down at me. But it wasn't a very nice smile. And it was as wide as a billboard.

One of those black leather pumps swung back and came right at me. I managed to roll over to the side before I got kicked. I crawled closer to the counter, which looked as tall as Mount McKinley. She brought her shoe down hard, trying to stomp on me. In the nick of time I jumped out of the way, or I'd have been served as the main course at a pancake supper. This baby wasn't fooling around. She was bent on homicide. She had drugged me with that cake and then that crumb of cheese. I knew it had something to do with Alice Wonderland. I had to find Alice and fast, before Mary Ann spread my willowy frame all over the lobby.

"Come here, I won't hurt you," she cooed, or screeched, because she sounded like a vulture in the top of a very tall tree. Her hand swept down and landed on the floor. It was the size of a trolley car. In her palm was a piece of chocolate cake as big as a truck tire.

She was a snake playing with me, a very small mouse, hoping I would scamper into her trap. On the floor near me lay a hatpin. It had a fake black pearl at one end and a needle sharp point. It fit my hand like a sword. Feeling like Errol Flynn in *The Sea Hawk*, I leaped toward the big, soft, white hand. I stabbed her thumb as hard as I could. She screamed like a fire truck. I dodged the gush of blood that poured out and kicked the cake out of her flapping mitt. Shearing off a piece with the hatpin sword, I bit into it. I figured it would make me disappear altogether or grow me bigger. Too bad there was no more cake.

Mary Ann was still howling about her thumb. I didn't like to get rough with skirts, but when they were trying to kill me with their high heels I stopped being a gentleman. I dashed around to the back of the counter and climbed up the chair leg. Her purse was on the seat. It was easy to climb in and check out the contents. One rod, some bullets, a lipstick, a pair of gloves, spectacles, a fan—and some cake. I scooped off some frosting with my finger and licked it. Nothing happened. I took a bite. Then another bite. I shot up a couple of feet.

"Ah ha!" she cried, poking her head over the counter and sucking on her bleeding thumb.

I knew I was in trouble. I used the hatpin to slice more cake and I jumped for the floor in the nick of time. She pushed the chair over and fell down, scrabbling for her purse. While she was getting untangled, I wolfed down the rest of the cake and hoped it was enough, or my goose was cooked.

The last gulp of cake exploded in my stomach. I shot up four more feet and towered over Mary Ann, who screeched and ran down the hall.

I let her go. That dame was bad news.

She had dropped a small lavender card on the carpet. I picked it up. It said EAT ME. I wasn't going to eat anything in this hotel again. I almost threw it away, but I flipped it over and looked at the other side. Someone had written *Mome Rath, Room 1865, Flamingo Hotel*, in flowery script. The card smelled like cheap perfume.

I put the clues together with lightning speed. That was where Mome Rath was holding Alice Wonderland prisoner. I drew my gat and got ready to shoot my way out of the lobby. But the doors were unlocked, so I stepped out on the sidewalk. It was dark. I must have been inside longer than I thought.

I trudged down the grimy, cracked pavement, on my way to the Flamingo Hotel. Up ahead I heard a newsboy hollering.

"Read all about it. Private Eye Wanted for Murder! Brown Derby Waiter Murdered!"

What? I pulled my fedora low over my eyes, threw a nickel at the boy and grabbed a paper. My mug was plastered all over the front page. Me, Jake Grimm, wanted for murder. I looked at the other picture. It was a grainy photograph of Joey Dormouse, sprawled out on the pavement. He had been gunned down in the alley behind the Brown Derby. Right after I'd questioned him about Alice. Everybody who worked at the Brown Derby had blabbed to the papers about how I'd socked Joey

Dormouse and slapped him around. I was headed for San Quentin unless I could find a way to clear myself.

I slipped into an alley and tried to think. I looked at the card again. Mome Rath must have murdered Joey Dormouse and set me up for the fall so I couldn't rescue Alice Wonderland from his clutches. The only way I could prove my innocence was to find Alice and get her away from that monster.

* * * *

I managed to dodge the cops and sneak over to the Flamingo Hotel without getting arrested. It was a swell joint. The tiles on the lobby floor looked like giant playing cards. It was like being in a casino.

The haughty broad at the desk flared her nostrils at me. "May I help you?" she sneered.

Women. You had to know how to handle them. "Don't do me any favors, sister. I'm looking for Alice Wonderland in Room 1865. Call her up and make it snappy."

The sourpuss dame showed her teeth. "There is no Alice Wonderland at this establishment. And we don't have a Room 1865. Now please leave before I call the hotel detective."

I didn't need to tangle with any hotel dicks. I knew the runaround when I heard it. Lucky for me, I was smarter than this old bat.

"Now, now. No need for that, sweetheart. I'm leaving," I said, giving her a grin. I sauntered toward the big double doors, but kept looking back over my shoulder. The dame started talking to another customer and I took my chance. I dashed toward the lush carpeted spiral staircase and ran upwards. Behind me I heard the clerk hollering for the hotel detective. Well, he'd have to catch me first.

I turned a corner and ran down the hallway. As I whizzed past, I heard a scream from behind one of the doors. I whirled around, drew my rod, and slammed my body into the door, which happened to be unlocked.

I rolled on the carpet and crashed into a writing desk. My rod went flying under the bed. I reached for it but someone's very big shoe stepped on my fingers. It hurt. A lot.

I looked up, up, up and kept on looking. I was looking at all six feet of Mome Rath, the scourge of the West Coast. He was a gorilla in a silk suit.

"Get your foot off me, buster. What have you done with Alice Wonderland?"

He pressed harder on my hand. I gritted my teeth. I'd show him he couldn't break me.

I broke. "Ow! Ow! Get off me!"

"Let him go, Momie," said a sweet, girlish voice.

Momie? I craned my neck back and saw an angel looking down at me. She had long blond hair and eyes like turquoise.

"Alice! You're Alice Wonderland," I said. "I've found you."

Mome Rath took his shoe off my hand and sat on the bed. "Okay, Alice. But just because you asked me," he said in a gravelly voice.

I got to my feet and brushed off my fedora. I was buying time. I had to get my gat from under the bed and save Alice from this hoodlum. I was gathering myself to make a leap, but Alice walked past me and sat on the guy's lap. She put her arms around his neck and gave him a big smooch, right on the kisser. I couldn't believe my eyes.

"What are you doing, Alice? This guy is the criminal mastermind of Southern California. You're a sweet young thing from the convent. You don't know what you're doing."

She smiled at me, her hair falling over one eye like Veronica Lake. "You sound like some hophead, mister. Momie is my husband. The only time I go to the convent is to visit my twin sister."

I goggled at her. "Twin sister?"

Blondie snuggled up to Mome Rath and patted his face. "Yeah, at the convent of Mucho Sur in Baja. Our folks got killed in a train wreck when we were babies. Sis became a novice, but I left as soon as I could and came to Hollywood. I was working in a nightclub when Momie saw me." She smooched her husband again. "And the rest, as they say, is history." She waved her left hand at me. She had on a diamond big enough to choke a bookie.

"I heard a scream."

She blushed. "Oh, Momie just gave me a diamond necklace for my birthday. I get so excited!" Huge, sparkling stones circled her neck. She was wearing enough baubles to start her own jewelry store.

My head was spinning. "How many Alices are there?"

"One Alice too many, Mr. Grimm," said a sultry voice behind me. I'd heard that voice before.

I whirled and saw my client. She was holding gats in both manicured hands. She smiled at me. "I figured if I followed you around I'd find her. You're such a buffoon you'd have to draw attention to yourself."

"Don't try to flatter me, sweetheart," I said, curling my lip. "It's time to come clean. Who are you?"

"She's my ex-wife," said Mome Rath, frowning at my client. "Her name's Red Duchess. She blew all the money I gave her on gambling and dope. She always wants more. She's been crazy jealous since I remarried, so I've tried to keep Alice hidden away from her."

"Now it all makes sense," I said, my brain working overtime. "You set me up, right from the start. You killed Joey Dormouse."

Red leveled her guns at my midsection. "I told you I met my sister at the Brown Derby because I knew you'd charge over there and make a fool of yourself. You have a reputation in this town. I also knew Joey Dormouse worked for Mome so I figured he'd call and let him know you were looking for Alice."

I gave her a steely glare. "You must have ambushed him in the alley and threatened to shoot him unless he told you where Alice was. But after the poor sap spilled his guts, you spilled his guts. You set me up for a fall, Red. But I'm too clever for you."

I whirled to look at Mome Rath. "When Joey told you a private dick was on Alice's tail, you got your operatives, the albino and the dame with the chocolate cake, to knock me in the head and dump me in the cellar of your sleazy hotel. What kind of chump do you take me for?"

Mome Rath shrugged. "Nothing personal, mister. I was so scared you'd track down Alice that I told Whitey and Mary Ann to cancel you out."

Red smirked at me. "I knew you'd make such a spectacle of yourself that Mome would do something stupid. And it worked. I found out where Mome's new wife is. I'll plug her like I plugged Joey Dormouse. No one takes my place."

"You'll go to the women's pen at Tehachapi for this, Red."

She shook her head. "No, not me. After the stunt you pulled downstairs in the lobby, you'll be nailed for the murder of Mome Rath and his child bride."

Mome Rath went pale and clutched Alice to him, but his arms wouldn't stop a bullet.

I was gathering myself to make a move when a nun walked into the room. The Flamingo was like Grand Central Station. No privacy.

"Can I help you, sister?" I said. She looked like Alice. The same gorgeous face. The same turquoise eyes. What was going on here?

The nun leaped forward and executed a perfect cartwheel, kicking Red in the puss with her little nun feet. Red dropped her rods and staggered backwards.

"Hey, look out," I shouted, but it was too late. Red fell out of the open window and smashed into the street below. Two cabs ran over her. Then a bakery truck. I turned away. The bakery truck really made a mess.

Alice and the nun embraced. Mome Rath was grinning ear to ear.

"Don't tell me," I said, taking out a cigarette. "You're Alice's twin sister from the convent. You must have got wind she was in trouble."

"My name's Dinah," said the nun. "When Red Duchess came down to Mucho Sur and said she was a long lost relative who was looking for me and Alice, I knew she was up to no good. We don't have any relatives left. There was something shifty about her. I had to find my sister in a hurry and warn her."

"Where did she get Alice's photograph?"

"Somebody broke into my office and took the picture," said Mome Rath. "I had it in a silver frame on my desk. That's when I moved Alice to a room here at the Flamingo. I knew something was wrong."

He reached in his wallet and handed me enough greenbacks to choke a horse. "Just so there's no hard feelings, fella."

I put the cash in my pocket and took a drag on my cig. "All's well that ends well," I said, blowing smoke rings up to the ceiling.

I winked at the nun. "You do a mean cartwheel, sister."

Dinah gave me a shy smile. "Alice and I used to do cartwheels all the time when we were growing up in the convent. We had so much fun. I'm glad I remembered how to do one. Although it's too bad Red Duchess died without confessing her sins."

"But she did. Red Duchess confessed to the murder of Joey Dormouse. It was a cartwheel in self-defense. Case closed, sister."

I straightened my fedora and strolled out of the Flamingo Hotel. It was time for this private dick, Jake Grimm, Hollywood P.I., to find my next case.

Like Red Duchess said, I had a reputation in this town.

THE WHEELS ON THE BUS GO ROUND AND ROUND

KAYE GEORGE

The small group lined up on the hot sidewalk to get onto my Jumbo-Bus that summer day in Knoxville. They didn't look much different from my normal passengers. But never in a million miles could I have told you what would happen with that bunch.

I drove up the slight hill and pulled to the curb where they all stood, waiting patiently. There was a black family with three young kids—I'd seen them before and thought the two girls were twins, cute as little ladybugs.

There's always college kids on the DC route. This time there were three of them. Two girls were traveling together, and the other one looked like a frat boy. He wasn't with them, but was hanging near, like he wanted to get to know them. Looked like he was a little older than the girls, maybe a senior or even a grad student.

Two middle-aged white ladies, all dolled up for the ride, wearing sundresses. Most people don't get fancy for a JumboBus ride, but a few do. They concentrated on their chatter so hard, I wasn't sure they'd seen the bus pull up.

Then there were three guys, all traveling alone. They were white, one maybe around the age of the ladies. The second one wore a suit and carried a briefcase, looked like a lawyer. The third looked like a bum. I thought about not letting the last one onto my bus. I would smell his breath and see how recent his last binge had been, and how much of it he had left in his system. Didn't need a drunk riling up the passengers.

I hopped out and opened the luggage compartment under the seats. Everyone had bags except the old stumble bum white guy. He carried a paper shopping bag with handles, but took it on the bus with him instead of letting me stow it below.

Taking up my station by the steps, I collected their reservation numbers as they filed on. It was going to be a beautiful, early spring day.

No rain in the forecast. Birds twittered in the small bushes next to the building. Should be an easy drive.

The family went up top so the kids could use the tables for games and coloring books. They'd been on my bus a few times. They had grandparents in the DC area and went to visit them now and then. Their last name was Holt, according to my list.

The older ladies in their sundresses were next. They both had blond hair, dyed to cover the gray. The one with short hair jangled the bangles on her wrist when she showed me her printout. The other one flicked her long hair back so her big hoop earrings danced just above her bare shoulders. She called the first one Sky. Her printout said Sky Meadows and the long-haired one's reservation said she was Brandi Bergman.

The two college girls, loaded down by their backpacks that looked to weigh forty pounds or so, barely looked up from their phones long enough to give me their reservation numbers, thumbs going like sports cars on the interstate. One was a blond honey—Tunisia Fish; the other— Mia Chang, was a cute little Asian.

Kelly Booke—I thought of him as Mr. Joe Cool—followed them. He held a phone, but his eyes were on the rump of the Asian college girl.

Then the three men got on, with the bum getting on last. His last drink of whiskey hadn't been very long ago, I'll tell you that. His hands shook and the whites of his eyes glowed red like a sunset. But he walked straight enough and he politely thanked me, although I hadn't done anything for him yet because he hadn't had any luggage. So I decided to let him on.

I climbed the steps and waited for the clock to say it was time to go, studying my load in my convex mirror.

Lawton Beane, the man dressed in a suit and carrying a briefcase, had taken a seat directly behind me, two rows back, leaving the first row vacant. The drunk staggered past him. The suit stared at him as he passed and I caught the suit mutter to him, "Still drunk, Stoney?"

"Still a stuffed shirt, Lawton?" The guy didn't sound extremely drunk.

No shit. The drunk's nickname was Stoney? I checked my manifest. Yep. Stoneham Sharp. The nickname fit, not the last name.

I pulled my microphone over and thumbed the switch. "Welcome to JumboBus. Our goal is to get you to Washington DC with as few wrecks as possible."

I usually got a few chuckles, so I paused. The "blond" ladies obliged me with some titters.

"The only problem we have is all those mountains between Knoxville and DC. Don't be alarmed if we slow down going up the mountain and speed up coming down. You can be alarmed if we run off the road, though."

The two backpack college girls had looked up and started paying attention after my first bit. The hanger-on college kid, taking his cue from them, watched me, too. He cracked a slight smile at my last funny. One of the girls smiled and shook her head.

"Departure is in about five minutes, so make yourselves comfortable. The restroom is that part of the bus that sticks out and has a door labeled 'restroom' in the middle there. Any time after we get going, feel free to use the facilities."

* * * *

All was quiet for the first fifty miles, except for the sounds of the kids upstairs, playing what sounded like a board game. Probably something on their parents' tablet. One of the little girls had a cute squeal when, it sounded like, she won or made a good move.

The suit, the one Stoney called Lawton, jumped up and clomped to the foot of the stairway.

"Can you keep those damn kids quiet up there?"

Everyone raised their heads to stare at him.

"Sir," I said, with my authoritarian voice, "take your seat."

"They're making too much damn noise."

"Sir, don't talk to children that way. If you can't ask them nicely, just take your seat."

"I'll ask them nicely, all right." He stomped up the stairs.

Before he could start hollering up there, I heard Mr. Holt's voice. It was quieter than Lawton Beane's had been but still clearly audible from my seat. "Do not curse in front of my children. I'll thank you to express yourself decently."

"Are you going to keep them quiet?"

"They're playing. Kids don't play without saying anything."

"I'm warning you!" I heard Lawton Beane clatter back down the stairs and watched him plop into his seat from my rear view mirror.

For the next fifty miles, the kids were quieter. Poor little tykes.

Kelly Booke, the college kid, had tried to engage the coed closest to him, the non-Asian one, in conversation. He'd gotten her name, Tuni, short for Tunisia, but was having trouble connecting much further than that. They'd gotten onto the subject of pets. Tuni said she kept rabbits and Kelly told her he'd had a dog when he was a boy, but a neighbor asshole had shot her. I could tell he was overplaying it, his voice getting an emotional quaver in the telling. I thought I even detected extra dampness in his eyes. It didn't work. She turned back to her phone and ignored him.

Beane's next victim was the frat boy, who sat across the aisle and back one seat. The college girls were behind Beane, so Joe Cool was across the aisle from them. Tiny, tinny sounds came from the kid's earbuds. I could barely hear it, but it wasn't bothersome.

Beane whirled in his seat to face the boy. "Shut that noise up. Why do you think the whole bus wants to listen to a song about some damn mutt?"

The kid had been smiling and nodding his head along with his tunes. I saw his face tighten after the attack. He fumbled for the controls and turned down the volume, looking daggers at Beane after he turned to face the front. Beane mumbled, loud enough to be heard by the girls behind him. "I suppose he's trying to impress those skanks. Why he'd want to do that is beyond me. Especially the fat skank." The kid didn't take his eyes off Beane for quite a few miles. I thought he was trying to drill a hole in the back of Beane's head with his dark look.

I started to consider putting Beane off the bus at the stop thirty miles ahead. Before we got there, he managed to sling more insults. One of the sundress women, the one with bangle bracelets, got up to use the restroom. She jiggled them down toward her wrist as she made her way up the aisle.

He turned to sneer at her. "Jesus Christ, woman. Why the hell would you want to advertise how cheap your junky jewelry is? Quit jingling like a sleigh bell."

The woman, Sky Meadows, stopped dead in her tracks. "What's wrong with you? Why are you bullying everyone? We're all complete strangers."

I thought Beane said something like, "Not complete." I studied the passengers. Stoney and Beane knew each other, unlikely as that was. I wondered if anyone else knew him.

Stoney Sharp had struck up a card game with the other male passenger, a guy with thick glasses named Clark Kenton. If you wanted to find someone to play the least likely Superman alter identity, it would be this guy. He was quiet and well-dressed and intent on the cards Stoney was dealing.

Beane turned around again and stared at Stoney. "Watch that guy," he said to Kenton. "He'll cheat. What are you losers playing anyway?"

Kenton looked at Beane with owl eyes through his lenses. "Draw poker."

Beane chuckled. "A game for losers." He turned to face the front and I could see his face. He was a sour, unhappy son of a bitch, that's for sure. I guess he wanted to make everyone else as miserable as he was. I decided I would definitely put him off at the half-way rest stop. I'd done it before with unruly passengers and I could do it again.

As we approached, I gave my talk about not leaving valuables on the empty bus, and warned them to be back in their seats in thirty minutes. I sat and filled out my paperwork, putting down distance and time, while the first of the passengers filed out. The two chatty women breezed past, then the two college girls, noses in their phones.

When my paperwork was done, I went to stand outside the door while the rest came off. The last to leave were the Holt family, the cute little girls skipping toward the concession building. The reason I was waiting was to tell Beane to make sure he had everything with him, since I wasn't letting him back on the bus. I hadn't noticed who had left and who hadn't and also had neglected to count heads, so I got back in and inspected. No one upstairs. No one down. Nothing was left in Beane's seat, so he must have gotten past me. I locked up and went to get my lunch.

My passengers milled around the place, getting snacks and burgers. The counter clerk had my usual ready and waiting for me, a pepperoni slice and a diet soda. I handed her the money, which included a nice tip. She gave me her usual million-dollar smile and I found a corner to wolf down my lunch. Beane didn't come into the small building unless he did it while I was in the john.

I was usually back in my seat in twenty minutes, counting heads as the passengers re-entered. Today, though, after I unlocked the door, I stood at the foot of the steps so I could intercept Mr. Lawton Beane. No way was I letting him back on my bus.

The two women, Sky Meadows and Brandi Bergman, were the first to return. As is always the case, they took the exact seats they'd had before. Next came Stoney Sharp and Clark Kenton. They seemed to have struck up a friendship. The Holt family clambered on board and the kids swarmed up the stairs. I could hear them singing, "The wheels on the bus go round and round." At the last minute, the three students ambled up, the two girls still absorbed in their electronics, the guy still eyeing their bottoms as they ascended the steps in front of him.

I waited five extra minutes. Mr. Beane was a no-show. Maybe he'd gotten past me and was stuck in the bathroom taking a dump. Not my problem. Now I wouldn't have to put him off the bus. I hopped up the stairs, closed the door, and took off.

The rest of the ride to DC was so much better. It was like my Jumbo-Bus breathed out a sigh of relief and settled into contentment. The kids sang and played upstairs, the two men played cards half the journey, then

Kenton leaned back for a nap and Stoney watched the scenery go by. The two young girls never quit playing with their phones. Mr. Joe Cool, across the aisle, seemed to have lost interest in them. He wasn't even wearing his earbuds, just staring out the window. The two middle-aged women chattered without restraint. It was a good ride. Right up until we were almost there.

The guy with the thick glasses, Clark Kenton, got up to use the bathroom. No one had used it since lunch. Kind of unusual, since people drank sodas and tea when we stopped.

I watched Clark get up and slowly navigate his way, on the rolling bus, to the door. The next time I glanced back in my mirror, he was standing in the aisle holding the door open, with a mighty strange expression on his face. His mouth and his eyes made perfect Os. He stood there for a few seconds. Then he slammed the door and ran up the aisle to me.

"There's... there's... he's on the floor... in the... he's not moving." He was whispering. Maybe he was afraid to say it too loud.

I frowned and put on my blinker. Someone must be sick, I thought. There happened to be a rest area in half a mile. I pulled off and stopped the bus. I announced that there was a slight problem, but we would be back on the road soon.

"Show me," I said, getting up and shooing Clark ahead of me. I had a bad feeling about what we'd find. Sure enough, I opened the door and Mr. Lawton Beane greeted me, sitting on the closed toilet lid, slumped against the wall, his tongue sticking out of his purple face.

I took a closer look, not wanting to touch anything. It looked like something was buried in the flesh of his neck. I stooped to get a better look. The guy had been killed. Strangled. The weapon was a cord with earbuds attached. Was it Joe Cool's? But why would he kill Beane? Anyone could have used his cord, I told myself. It didn't have to be the college kid.

I had to keep all the passengers on the bus until the police arrived. One of them was a killer. I announced that we would have to spend some time at this rest area, then I went to the front and quietly called the cops.

Mr. Holt came down the stairs. "Can I let the kids out to run around?"

"I'm sorry, Mr. Holt. I have to keep everyone on the bus."

A collective groan went up at that news.

"What the problem?" asked Brandi Bergman.

"I'm not at liberty to—"

"That asshole guy is dead in the bathroom!" yelled Kenton.

They all started yammering at once.

I held up both my hands, palms out. "Calm down, everyone. The police are on their way. As soon as they have a look and release the vehicle, we'll get back on the road." I was lying. I'd had a murder on my bus once before, years ago, and I knew we'd be here for a good long time.

One college girl, Mia, stood up. "I have a test tomorrow."

"Me, too," said Kelly Booke, Mr. Joe Cool.

"We won't be here all night," I said, as reassuringly as I could. "Relax. Just pretend we're still on the road."

"But, but," stammered Brandi Bergman, shaking so that her hoop earrings trembled next to her neck, "there's a dead guy? In the bathroom?"

"It's the asshole," Kenton helpfully repeated.

"He just died there?" "What is he dead of?" "Are you gonna call someone?" "Are you sure he's dead?"

"Yes," I said. I might as well tell them. "Mr. Lawton Beane has expired and he's in the bathroom."

"Ha, expired," said Stoney Sharp. "It's about time his expiration date came due."

"Couldn't have happened to a nicer guy," said Brandi's companion, Sky.

"Did anyone see him go into the bathroom?" I asked. It had to have been before the stop. They shook their heads in unison. "Did you see anyone at all go in there within, maybe, twenty or thirty miles of our stop?"

"We were waiting for the rest area bathroom," Brandi said.

"Us too, right, Tuni?" Mia spoke and Tuni, her friend, nodded.

Mr. Joe Cool shrugged. Stoney stared out the window. I knew Mr. Holt had been upstairs. No one had seen anything?

* * * *

The cops got there in record time. Luckily, no one had tried to force their way off the bus. I didn't know what I would have done if they had.

They questioned all of us separately, pulling everyone off the bus two or three at a time. When my turn came, the policewoman asked me if I'd seen him get off the bus. I thought for a moment. The only thing I could say was the truth. No, I hadn't. I told her I had locked the bus at the half-way stop and he must have been already dead then because he definitely didn't get back on.

She continued to ask me some more questions about the passengers, like had I noticed any friction. Yes, with everyone. Had I noticed that anyone on the bus knew him? I hesitated only a moment, but had to tell her that Stoney Sharp had obviously been acquainted with Mr. Beane.

"How do you know?"

"They traded insults right off the bat. I mean, Beane insulted every-one, but he said something about Sharp, like, was he still drinking. And Sharp, I remember, asked Beane if he was still a stuffed shirt."

"Did you recognize the weapon?"

I hesitated. "It's from a set of ear buds. But I couldn't say whose."

She wrote in her notebook, flipped it shut, and told me I could get back onto the bus.

"Excuse me, but do you know how much longer we'll be here? I can call another bus to take the passengers on to DC if it will be a long time."

She cocked her head and considered. "Ask me in an hour. Can you do that?"

I didn't want to, but an hour wasn't too much of a delay. Hell, we sometimes were delayed an hour because of traffic.

When Stoney Sharp's turn came, they kept him out of the bus for a long time. The sun had set some time ago and a chill wind picked up. It puffed in through the door every time I opened it to let someone off or on.

Finally, everyone had been interrogated. The one who seemed to be in charge, a big bull of a guy in a gray suit, knocked on the door and I admitted him. He stood at the front, silent, eyeballing the passengers with a steely gaze. "Mr. Sharp?" His voice was soft, but gruff.

Stoney Sharp jumped up. The homicide cop motioned him to the front with a jerk of his head.

"Look, that high school stuff was a long time ago," Stoney said, standing beside his seat.

Mr. Cop dangled a pair of handcuffs. "Come forward, Sharp."

"No, I didn't kill him. I wanted to, long ago. Lawton made sure I took some of the drugs he was dealing the day the football scout came to our high school game. I missed out of the scholarship. I blamed him for years, but I didn't kill him."

"Get over here." Mr. Cop's voice was getting louder.

"Can I say something?" I asked. "Outside?"

He squinted at me, but followed me off the bus for a one on one.

"What was that around Beane's neck?"

"A cord."

"But was it a headphone cord? Were there earbuds on the end of it?"

He didn't answer.

"One of my passengers might be missing a set of earbuds." Much as I hated to, I had to mention it. Joe Cool hadn't used his since the stop.

They pulled the kid, Kelly Booke, off the bus. I watched through the window as Kelly gestured and protested as hard as he could. At the end of the discussion, the policewoman slapped the handcuffs on him.

I opened the door and stepped down. "What was that about?" I asked the homicide detective.

"Booke says he recognized Beane pretty soon after the ride started. Beane shot his dog when he was a little boy. He's never forgotten. He said that Beane had only gotten meaner and nastier over the years. He's been looking for him for a long time. When his chance came, he took it."

"When did he do it?"

"Beane went to the john and didn't lock the door. Booke followed him in and surprised him. Strangled him from behind. Didn't think anyone saw or heard. They were all absorbed in themselves, he said. He made a full confession. Don't tell anyone I told you this." He gave me his hard look. "I'll deny it. But it's your bus. You should know. And you'd better call a backup. Crime Scene is going to have to go over this vehicle."

I was surprised two people fit in the bathroom. Joe Cool, Kelly Booke, must have been determined. The voices of the little girls floated down from the top of the bus, singing, "The wheels on the bus go round and round." So did the wheels of justice, I reflected. They crushed both Lawton Beane and Kelly Booke, poor bastard.

BUON VIAGGIO

LAURA OLES

Mary Campisi leaned over the gas burner, inspecting a simmering pot partially filled with *al pomodoro*, or, as the rest of her family referred to it, spaghetti sauce.

"Just because you married an Italian doesn't mean you have to completely drink the Kool-Aid," Irene said. Mary's mother had watched her daughter slowly shed the skin of her Irish heritage in favor of her husband's Italian background since she had eloped with him in secret last year.

"You mean drink the Italian soda. Kool-Aid is so… inferior," Kathleen said in a faux Italian accent. Her disdain for her baby sister's whole-hearted embrace of all things Italian rolled smoothly off her tongue.

Mary shook her head, her eyes trained on the sauce as she stirred. "There's nothing wrong with wanting to learn to cook like Marco's mother. Besides, who doesn't love Italian food?"

"Your sister has a point," Irene said. "Just don't forget the importance of your own heritage. To listen to that husband of yours go on about how superior Italians are… well, he makes the French sound humble." Irene's words hung in the air as she turned her attention toward the crisper drawer in the refrigerator. Leaning over the coldbox, she muttered, "Now where is that Romaine, anyway?"

Irene had pulled the lettuce from the drawer when the sound of the back door drew her attention. Marco, Mary's new husband, emerged and walked through the back room to the connecting kitchen. He surveyed his in-laws with his signature indifference and simply said, "*Ciao*," to no one in particular. He then made a beeline for the refrigerator, where Irene still stood holding her Romaine, and pulled a bottle of Merlot from the shelf. His face twisted in an animated display of disgust.

"Merlot *non dovrebbe essere freddo*," he said to his wife.

"*Sono d'accordo*," she replied to him, her eyes still focused on the sauce as if she preferred not to make eye contact with anyone in the room. "Merlot isn't supposed to be cold, Mom."

Irene shrugged. "Oh, I see. And Marco couldn't tell me that in English? He seems to speak it just fine in public." Her eyes locked on Marco but he kept his gaze elsewhere, as if unwilling to answer his mother-in-law's challenge.

Marco left the bottle on the counter top untouched and, without his evening wine, retired to his regular seating place in the next room. Putting his feet up in a leather recliner, he stretched out like a satisfied cat, exhaling audibly while placing his hands behind his head.

Kathleen peered into the next room at her brother-in-law, her annoyance clear from her narrowed eyes and audible sighs. She knew he could hear every word from the next room but she raised her voice for his benefit anyway. "He loves that we don't understand what he's saying. That's why he does it. And why is it that he knows exactly when to show up for dinner but doesn't have the decency to sit in the same room?" She turned to her sister. "You let him walk all over you, you know. You might as well have 'Welcome' written on your chest."

Mary shrugged. "He's just different, you know? Different cultures, different expectations."

Kathleen wasn't buying it but she lowered her voice for only immediate family's ears. "I thought Italians were talkative and friendly. He acts like Mom's grumpy Uncle Walter. That man sucked the joy out of every room as soon as he walked in."

"Don't mess with an Irish mother," Irene said with the hint of a grin. She looked at Mary and noticed the forced smile on her face. "Honey, I know you're in a tough position when he acts like this but you really should say something to him. It's causing a lot of friction in the family and now that he wants to be part of the family business...."

"Which isn't happening." Garrett Murphy, the only son and eldest child in the Murphy family, had arrived just in time to add his two cents to the weekly discussion regarding why Marco was such an ass and how Mary should fix it.

Garrett loosened the navy and silver striped tie around his neck by working it left and right with his forefinger hooked around the knot. He would have certainly been voted "Least Likely to Wear a Tie" if the category had existed in high school, but their mother's desire to have him run the family business had been a strong motivation for him to dress like a respectable grownup.

Garrett glanced through the open cutout window that connected the living room and the kitchen. "His Italian Majesty has graced us with his presence, I see." He dropped his tie on a nearby table and walked the few steps toward his mother, who had been nursing a hot toddy. "You can't bring him into the business, Mom," he said simply. He then looked to his baby sister, Mary. "No offense. I mean, the bar is one thing, but the other thing? That's blood family only."

Mary remained in her fixed stirring position over the pot, now tending to the boiling Fusilli noodles. She took the saltshaker and tipped it over the boiling water, the addition creating frothy foam in the bubbling water. "Give him a chance, Garrett."

"The man doesn't make any effort to be involved in this business and you want us to bring him into the most important aspect of our family just because he married you? By convincing you to elope so your family had no say? We should trust him now?"

Irene had given her three children what the kids called the "Marry Right" speech upon each child's high school graduation and reminded her offspring that their choice of spouse would be the most important decision they would ever make. It would affect the entire family.

Irene's parents fought throughout her childhood, the events often ending in drunken tirades and physical abuse. Irene's own mother, Katy, finally left her husband under the cover of darkness with nothing more than her five children, a single suitcase, and the money she'd skimmed from her weekly grocery trips. Given her upbringing, Mama Irene had earned the right to counsel her kids on matters of the heart and she had made certain to choose an honorable man as her husband. Unfortunately, Mary had fallen for an unemployed Italian playboy who looked to his wife for financial support.

And the entire family was now paying the price.

Mary walked to the step that joined the kitchen and the living room and said to her husband. "*La cena è pronta.*" He rose as he did each night when she told him dinner was ready and walked to the kitchen. Mary prepared a plate for him, which he accepted with an expression that indicated he wasn't impressed. He raised his eyebrows as if he was puzzled by what occupied his plate. Saying nothing, he carried the plate back to the living room to dine in the pleasure of his own company.

Kathleen muttered something about an ungrateful ass underneath her breath while the rest of the family busied themselves with retrieving plates and utensils. Irene helped herself to a generous helping of pasta and sauce. "It looks wonderful, Mary. Thank you for making dinner."

"Yeah, thanks, sis," Garrett said, his own plate waiting to be filled.

Mary smiled. Her shoulders relaxed and she nodded in response.

"*Tagliatelle sono stracotte,*" Marco called out.

The smile fell from her face. She asked her mother. "Are the noodles overcooked?"

Irene took a bite of pasta and shook her head. "Absolutely not. Perfect *al dente*." She then reached for a squat bottle of Kilbeggan Irish whiskey and used a heavy hand to refresh her drink.

"Going to be one of those evenings, eh, Mom?" Kathleen quipped, signaling her to pass the bottle, which Irene obliged by sliding it across the granite center island. Garrett took a bar stool seat next to Kathleen. "Why don't you pour me one of those?"

Kathleen stood and retrieved another glass from a nearby cabinet and held one up for Mary. "Want me to pour you one?"

Mary considered it for a moment. "I'll just stick with wine, thanks."

Kathleen shrugged, filled the two glasses with ice and placed them in front of her seat and Garrett's next to her. "Nothing a little Kilbeggan can't fix, just like Grandma used to say." Kathleen, Irene and Garrett all raised glasses in the air.

"*Slainte!*" they proclaimed in unison.

The four family members ate at the bar, sharing small talk about the day's events and exchanging the latest gossip. Irene mentioned how she'd heard that Mrs. Donovan was finally considering selling her building in downtown Austin.

"That would be the perfect place for us," Garrett said. "We've talked about it before, but I never thought she'd sell. I thought she'd be buried in that building, the way she went on about it."

Irene polished off her drink. "It seems that Gibby left a lot of debt after he died and this is the only way for her to pay it off. She looks like she's aged ten years since he passed."

The conversation stopped as Marco returned to the kitchen, his plate showing most of the pasta remaining on the plate. Mary glanced at the subtle rejection of her cooking, and kept her eyes on her own food as he placed the dish on the counter.

He held out his hand. "*Dammi le chiavi.*"

Mary reached into her pocket and handed him a small key ring containing a Porsche emblem. He then placed a second set of keys in front of her. She looked to her mom. "I had Danny take a look at Marco's car to do a little tune up. It was making a funny noise."

"Danny's the best. Did he give you the family discount?"

"Of course. I don't pay full price for anything."

Mary returned to her meal while Marco said nothing. The kitchen remained silent as he walked toward the back door leading outside. He called over his shoulder, "*Buonanotte!*" and closed the door behind him.

The rest of the family returned to their dinner.

"*Buonanotte*, dickhead," Garrett huffed as he crammed a large fork full of pasta in his mouth. He looked over at Mary.

"Something's got to change, sis. He joins our family business over my dead body."

* * * *

"Mary, why don't you ever go out with him?" Irene asked, her hands now busy with the evening's dinner dishes. She placed the pasta bowls inside the dishwasher and closed the door. Grabbing a nearby towel, she dried her hands. "Don't you get tired of staying home alone?"

Mary shook her head but her expression was in clear conflict with her words. "Not really. He likes to spend time with his Sicilian friends and my Italian isn't good enough to follow their conversation. I'd just sit there confused about what they're talking about."

"You mean, like the way we do when he comes over for dinner and refuses to speak English?" Garrett's words carried more than a hint of sarcasm.

"All of this piling on isn't helping Mary so let's give it a rest," Irene said. She tried to lighten the mood. "What's the old saying? If you want praise, die. If you want blame, marry."

Mary cracked a smile. She nodded. "Very, very true."

Garrett remained unamused. "Maybe if she'd stand up to him a bit, he'd change his behavior. Why should we cater to his rudeness? He shows up just in time to eat our food, makes some comment that we can't understand because he doesn't have the balls to say it in English, and then leaves. It's bullshit."

The smile fell from Mary's face and she continued to busy herself with wiping the counters. Irene shot a glare at her eldest child, who responded by shrugging. "What?" he mouthed to her. Kathleen kept her post at the dishwasher, appearing enthralled with making sure that each plate was perfectly lined up in the bottom rack. Garrett walked over to his sister and put his arm around her. "I'm sorry. He doesn't treat you right and I hate having to stand here and watch it."

Mary nodded, leaning into his hug but not returning it. She folded the dishtowel and left it on the counter. "I'm going to head home. Still have some chores to do before I go to bed."

The back door creaked, announcing that someone else had arrived.

"I'm home! Someone get me a beer immediately." Connor Murphy looked around at the somber family faces in the kitchen. "What did I just walk into?"

Irene smiled at her husband. "Marco. As usual."

Connor grimaced but added nothing to the conversation. Kathleen retrieved a beer from inside door of the fridge and handed it to him. He checked the label before taking a sip. "Thank God we still have some

Guinness in the house." He reached inside his pocket and pulled a bottle opener from it. He had the top off in an instant and took a long draw from the beer bottle.

Kathleen chided her father. "You've got to quit bringing those openers home from the pub, Dad. We have about twenty of them in the kitchen drawer already. Keeping expenses down, remember?"

Connor held his beer up in response. "That's my little penny pincher. Glad we've got you handling the books." He looked at his youngest daughter. "You okay?"

Mary nodded. "Sure, Dad." She hugged her mom who was still standing by her side. "I'm going to go. Marco should be home soon."

Garrett muttered under his breath, "Yeah, right."

Irene doled out another stern stare at her son. Kathleen waved good-night to her sister and they all watched Mary disappear out the back door.

The four remaining family members gathered at the kitchen table. Irene chastised her son. "You aren't helping things by giving Mary a hard time. She can't control him. She's not strong enough."

Garrett disagreed. "She doesn't like confrontation and he knows it. Don't you hate the way he smirks at us and rubs our noses in it? He knows we're going to keep the peace and he uses it against us."

Kathleen tapped her fingers on the table. "This is why she's not involved in the business. She doesn't have the backbone. I wish she did, but she doesn't." Almost to herself she added, "I still don't understand how she can have our genes and always cower from an argument."

Irene rested her hand on her husband's forearm. "Honey, I know you have this dream of all the kids being involved but I don't think that's going to happen. Mary's choice in husbands has complicated things. Maybe our life isn't for her. Our life isn't for most people."

Garrett leaned back in his chair. "Well, we've got another problem with Marco, aside from his attitude."

Katherine threw her hands in the air. "Now what?"

"Marco said that he'd heard from a reliable source that Frankie Mann and his crew do a lot of business at Murphy's. He said he'd hate for the cops to hear such things but that he'd keep quiet if he were brought into the business."

Connor slammed his hand down on the table. "Does he have any idea who he's dealing with?" He stood up from the table, walking to the kitchen counter. "I don't want to talk about that leech right now. I'm starving. What's left?"

"Spaghetti," Katherine offered in a dry tone.

"I'm sick of Italian. Food, people, all of it."

Irene worked to calm her husband. She followed him to the kitchen. "Let me make you a sandwich. It's going to be fine. Marco doesn't know anything more than rumors."

Garrett rubbed his eyes. The day had worn long. "He said he had proof, but I don't know how. He's not involved at the pub for anything more than drinking away our profits." He considered the possibility for a moment. "Unless he's been snooping around our office without us knowing, but I don't see how. Everyone knows the office is off limits to everyone but family."

Katherine continued her finger tapping on the table. "Frankie Mann isn't going to cross us. He needs us more than we need him."

Irene put the finishing touches of mustard on a salami hoagie for her husband and handed it to him on a glass plate. "Eat this and calm down. We'll handle it."

"Damn straight." Garrett's mounting frustration encompassed him like a hive of angry bees. The Murphy men were known to be quick to anger and long to forgive, holding a grudge closer than even a dear friend.

Irene returned to the family table and sat next to her son. "Don't get yourself all worked up. It clouds your judgment. And besides, this family has seen far worse than the likes of Marco." She glanced at her husband. "I have a feeling that this situation will work itself out soon enough. Isn't that right, Connor?"

Connor nodded. "Yes, I have a feeling it will."

* * * *

Murphy's happy hour was happy indeed. The main bar, which had been brought over from Ireland from a pub with a hundred year history, was the focal point of the establishment. Rarely was more than a stool or two open at any given time. The stools were coveted perches with the best views of the big-screen TVs, not to mention the waitresses.

At this moment, Connor Murphy was in full entertaining mode. He was a gifted storyteller, entertaining his patrons with tales of growing up in Ireland with his boisterous family. Murphy had even regaled his guests with stories of brawls and bribes that took place in Flannery's Pub, the place from which the Murphy's carved wood bar had originated. It came with two attachable wait wells, countless Celtic carvings on its surface and enough stories to keep Connor's lips moving—and customers drinking—well into the evening.

At this particular moment, Connor was behind the bar serving drinks to a group of three businessmen wearing button-down shirts and khaki pants, their union resembling a meeting of Red Lobster wait staff. The clock celebrated happy hour with a loud bong announcing it was now 5:00 p.m., and the doors hosted a steady stream of work-weary stiffs looking to take a load off.

Garrett emerged from the office, which was tucked away in the back of the building, close to the bathrooms and the storage closet. He closed the door behind him, checking the knob to ensure the door had locked. He made a beeline for the bar where his father continued to share scotch and stories.

"Looks like you're keeping busy, Dad," Garrett said as he slipped behind the bar to join his father.

"If you're going to take up space back here, you'd better be working."

Garrett's hands had already traveled to the shot glasses before his father had finished his sentence. He knew the drill. He began serving drinks on his eighteenth birthday and knew at that moment that he would one day take over the management of Murphy's Pub.

Garrett then glanced over and noticed something unappealing in the doorway.

Marco.

He strode casually to the bar and nodded at Garrett and Connor, taking a seat at an open stool between a corporate suit and a UPS delivery driver. His polished clothing, expensive watch and perfectly managed mane were a stark contrast to the men flanking him on each side of the bar. A Baptist minister would have blended in better.

Connor and Garrett busied themselves until they caught up with customer drink requests. Marco waved his hand in the air, a twenty-dollar bill folded lengthwise between his fingers. "I'll have a glass of Merlot, not from the fridge," he said, dropping the money on the bar.

Garrett took the twenty off the bar and turned his back to Marco. He retrieved a bottle of Merlot from a small wine shelf. He filled the glass exactly half-full and placed it in front of Marco, not making eye contact.

Marco studied the wine. "Glassware looks a little dirty," Marco said, his voice evenly laced with a hint of condescension.

Garrett held up the glass to his own inspection. "It's perfect, as always. Your criticism doesn't have any power over me like it does over Mary, so feel free to shut the hell up."

Connor was serving draft beers to three nearby patrons but his smile revealed he had heard the exchange between his son and son-in-law.

Marco appeared nonplussed. "My opinion should matter. I believe, as a member of the business, I could be quite valuable."

Garrett laughed at the comment. Taking note of the patrons nearby, he leaned in, closing the space between he and Marco. He whispered,

"Valuable doing what? You've shown you excel at mooching off my family and getting my sister to believe your shit doesn't stink, and I don't see how either of those skills would benefit anyone here."

Marco stood up from the bar stool. His wine glass remained untouched, a signal that the Murphy offering was beneath him. As always.

"I have a feeling you'll change your mind soon," Marco said as he straightened his neatly pressed white shirt into his equally neatly pressed dress slacks.

Garrett noticed one thing was missing. "No wedding ring, eh? I guess you just forgot to put it on."

Marco said nothing, and instead, continued walking toward the door.

"Nice to see you again, Marco." A pretty waitress sporting a ponytail and a Murphy's T-shirt and jeans nodded to him as he walked out the front door.

Connor signaled her over. "Jen, what do you mean, again? When was Marco here?"

Jen slipped her order pad in the waitress apron fastened around her waist. "He was here earlier today. He went into the office to get something he needed. Is that okay? I thought it was okay for him to be in there."

Connor's expression hardened. "Uh, it's fine, Jen. Thanks. Go ahead and get that back table. Don't want them to wait too long."

Jen nodded and left to take care of the group. Connor called his son over and whispered in his ear.

"We might have a problem. Marco was in our office."

Garrett moved swiftly from the bar toward the office. He unlocked the office door and then closed it behind him. He returned two minutes later, his expression stern. He leaned to whisper into his father's ear. "Last month's log book is missing."

* * * *

It was Thursday night and Mary retreated to her weekly routine of trying to busy herself in her living room cleaning out desk drawers and organizing receipts while waiting for Marco to appear from the bedroom. After an hour of male primping, Marco emerged.

Her husband loved to make an entrance. His cologne reached her before he did, and he flashed a smile that was almost as bold as the cobalt blue shirt he had paired with jeans so tight they flirted with the imagination.

"You look like you're ready to take on the town," Mary said, accepting Marco's embrace with little enthusiasm. She buried her face in his neck.

He kissed her forehead. "Just the usual friends, my love. Nothing for you to worry about."

"Maybe I should go with you," Mary offered. She brushed her hair from her face, the loose strands escaping from a messy ponytail. "It wouldn't take but a minute for me to get ready."

Marco's eyes met hers and he kissed her again. "You never like to go, you know that. Your Italian needs to be better. Then you'll have fun." He gave her a pat that felt more like pity than passion. "I know how you like to stay in with your tea and your books. You relax here and I'll be home later." He released her and walked toward the desk. "Where are my keys? I know I left them here."

Mary reached into her sweater pocket and held them up. "Here they are."

He grinned at her. "Trying to keep me home, eh?" He held his hand out to receive them. Mary held them for another moment before dropping them into his care.

"I know I could never do that. No, I left my sunglasses in your car and I needed them back. I have to be on the road early tomorrow to finish Mr. Bean's inventory audit and you know how bad the sun is on my drive into town. Almost blinding some mornings."

Marco nodded as she spoke but Mary could see his attention had already left in anticipation of spending an evening out. He adjusted his shirt and his sleeves and stole a glance at himself in a nearby mirror hanging on the wall. Mary retreated to the living room couch and picked up a book from the coffee table. She had already prepared the table with a bottle of Merlot and her favorite wine glass. She began pouring her consolation prize as Marco made his way out for the evening.

"*Avere un bon tempo,*" she called out to him as he walked toward the front door. He looked over his shoulder and rewarded her with one of the smiles that had once convinced her to ignore those nagging doubts about where he spent his evenings.

"Have a good time," she said again, picking up her glass and holding it in the air in toast. Marco closed the door behind him, leaving his wife to enjoy her own company for yet another night.

Mary told herself she'd wait at least an hour before she picked up the phone. At the forty-five minute mark, she couldn't stand it any longer.

"Hey, it's me."

"Hey, me. How are you doing?"

"Sitting on the couch alone again." Mary sighed. "You want to give me the big sister lecture about being a doormat?"

Kathleen laughed. "I was going to say something about seeing 'Welcome' written on your chest, but I know you've heard that one before."

Mary finished the wine in her glass and quickly poured herself another. She wondered how many glasses Marco had finished by now and if he was pouring drinks for anyone… else.

"Why am I not enough?" Mary asked, her voice picking up just the hint of a whine at the end. "He never wants me to go out with him and his friends. My Italian is getting better but he still says no. He acts like he's doing me a favor but I know he doesn't want me there."

Kathleen remained quiet on the other end of the line. Finally, Mary broke the silence. "Do you think there's someone else?"

Her question was met with a minute of silence. "Mary? Are you alright?"

She sniffed away the tears she'd been talking herself out of since her husband had chosen his friends over her. Again. "It's okay. I mean, it's not okay, but… you know what I mean."

More of what Mary had been holding in began spilling out. "It's all the cliché stuff of perfume and makeup on his shirt, but he says it's just from hugging his friends at the club. Nothing to worry about, he tells me."

"And do you believe that?"

"I don't know what I believe. I know you think he's a rat, so you don't have to pretend."

Kathleen let a small laugh slip. "You never did listen to me anyway."

"I know I have a problem, but I have to fix it myself."

"You know we can help you… with things."

Mary sighed into the phone. "I know, but Dad can be a bit heavy-handed sometimes."

"You mean that thing at the place last year?"

"His calling card can be easy to spot if you know what to look for. I need to talk to him about that. It's going to get him into trouble one of these days."

"Well, I can come over if you need me to."

Mary reached for her wine glass but decided against opening another bottle. Getting drunk wouldn't cure her loneliness.

"Thanks for the offer, but I think I'd rather be alone. I'm getting used to it."

On second thought, maybe she'd open another bottle after all.

* * * *

The ringing phone jarred Mary off the couch from a deep sleep. She looked around the room, disoriented at first, trying to remember where she'd put the cordless phone. She glanced at the clock hanging over the bookshelf. It was now after two in the morning. She didn't have an answering machine, so the trill of the phone continued. She felt around the couch cushions, now crumpled from her restless wine-induced nap. After more fumbling, she located the receiver wedged between two pillows.

"Hello?"

"Hello. This is Officer Clark with the Austin Police Department. Who am I speaking to?"

Mary rubbed her head, still a bit flushed from waking up so abruptly. "This is Mary Campisi. Uh, is everything okay?"

"Ma'am, I'm sorry but there's been a car accident involving a Marco Campisi. Is that your...."

"Husband," she said, her voice barely audible.

"We have a car on the way to your home, ma'am. An officer will be there very soon."

Mary said nothing further and hung up the phone, dropping the handset on the floor as she curled up into the couch in the fetal position and waited for the doorbell to ring.

* * * *

Mary sat on a bar stool nursing a glass of whiskey. Murphy's had been officially closed for hours but, when it came to family emergencies, it remained the first place the clan gathered in a crisis.

Kathleen slid onto the barstool next to her younger sister. The wood creaked as she shifted her weight and scooted the stool closer. "I'm so sorry about what happened," she said, putting her arm around her grieving sibling. Mary said nothing, simply hanging her head while stifling back an occasional sob. She hadn't cried much in the car since the officer had left her home. It didn't seem real just yet, that he was gone.

Garrett stood behind the bar in the corner, his arms crossed and at a loss for words. "I can't remember the last time this family was so quiet," Garrett joked. He often used humor to lighten tense situations but this time his efforts fell flat.

Kathleen gave her sister's hand a squeeze. "You know we're here for you, don't you? You know how we felt about him, but we really just wanted you to be happy."

Mary rubbed her eyes and released her sister's hand in favor of finishing her whiskey. It was gone in one quick throwback. She set the glass down gently and signaled to her mom for another one.

"You sure, sweetie? You're usually a two wine-glass kind of girl."

"Well, it's not every day you become a widow, right?"

Irene reached over the bar and stroked Mary's hair. "I'm so sorry, honey." Never one to linger too long with somberness, Irene turned her attention to pouring her daughter another whiskey. It was the family crutch for troubles and heartbreaks, and while it didn't cure anything, it kept them at a distance.

Garrett finally moved from the back corner of the bar, walking through the wait well's opening so he could be next to his sister. "You know I didn't like Marco, and I certainly didn't like how he tried to blackmail us with his threats, but I am sorry that you're going through this." He held Mary close. She slumped into the safety that was her brother's embrace.

Kathleen added, "I know Marco liked to drive fast on Ranch Road 2222, but that's tough to drive sober, let alone…"

Mary finished her sister's sentence, "…if you're drunk." She downed her second shot. "He played fast and loose… with a lot of things, I know that. It just took me awhile to get brave enough to do something about it."

Connor and Irene locked eyes.

Mary signaled to her mom for another shot.

Kathleen asked, "What do you mean by that?"

Mary remained still, cradling her head in her hands. "I mean, even I can be pushed too far."

She reached down on the ground for her handbag, pulling it up by the shoulder straps. Cradling it in her lap, she fished around inside and pulled out a small brown journal decorated with a gold-embossed M in the bottom right-hand corner.

Irene recognized it immediately.

"How on Earth did you get that?"

"I heard him on the phone talking about our… business. In Italian. My comprehension is much better than I let on." She touched the journal. "I took it out of his car yesterday before he left for the club."

Garrett exchanged glances with his father.

Mary slid the book across the bar to her mother's hand. "You can put this back in the office where it belongs. He never should have taken it, shouldn't have stolen my keys to the office. He never should have thought he could blackmail my family that way. My weakness made him think those things were all his right."

Mary's face now showed shades of hardness, like a child who realized there really were monsters in the world far more dangerous than in any storybook.

She downed her third whiskey and placed the glass on the bar with force. "He depended on me to take care of everything for him, even his precious sports car. I guess I needed to take care of myself this time."

Garrett remained silent.

Irene looked to her daughter.

"Maybe Mary is ready for the family business after all."

APORKALYPSE NOW

GALE ALBRIGHT

My husband was in the garage playing with one of his things.

"Fred, why don't you quit playing with those things and come in to dinner?" I asked, sticking my head around the laundry room door. "I fixed some real nice pork chops."

"Quit calling them things," he said. "They're bicycles."

He was sitting in front of his red bicycle with a toothbrush in his hand.

I laughed. "What are you doing, brushing its teeth?"

"I'm cleaning the wheel spokes. They get road film when I ride." He dipped the brush in a bucket of sudsy water and kept stroking those spokes.

"Why don't you use the hose? That'll take all night. The chops will get cold."

"I want to finish this. You go ahead without me."

I shut the door and went back to the kitchen. The golden-brown pork chops, the black-eyed peas swimming in bacon, the buttery, garlicky mashed potatoes all just sat there, turning to ice.

He could be such a jerk. It would serve him right if I sat down and ate the whole dinner all by myself and left Mr. Bicycle Thing to starve. He had four bikes. Was he going to clean them all tonight?

An hour and forty-five minutes later, well after dark, Fred came in the house. He was filthy, as usual, after playing with his things. Excuse me, *bicycles*.

"Well, did you finish brushing the bicycle's teeth? Did it need some mouthwash, too?"

He didn't answer me. I was sitting in my recliner, trying to watch my favorite reality show. He made a bunch of noise in the sink, splashing around, using that Lava soap he kept by my liquid Dawn.

"If you're looking for dinner, I put it up. I was afraid it would go bad," I said. "It is summer, you know."

"Yeah. And you keep this house freezing with the air conditioning, so what's the difference? We might as well be living in the Arctic."

I gritted my teeth and decided to play nice. "You want me to microwave you some dinner?"

Fred shook his head and dried off his filthy arms with one of my mother's best dish towels.

"No, I'll have a power shake. I'm not really that hungry. I keep telling you, pork's bad. Too much fat clogs your arteries. I want to quit eating meat."

The four pork chops I'd eaten rumbled in my stomach. Quit eating meat!

It was that damn bike riding that put these crazy ideas in his head. Ever since he started reading bicycle magazines he'd talked about going vegetarian. He e-mailed me articles from so-called health experts. They told you to drink ninety quarts of water a day, pump iron, and eat brown rice.

Fred proceeded to grind up frozen blueberries, flax meal, yeast, lecithin, and soy milk in the blender, ruining the climax of my show with all that crunching and whirring. Then he strolled in with a brimming glass of foamy pink stuff, sat in his recliner and promptly changed the channel.

"What are you doing? Cherie is about to tell all the other girls how Mona is messing around with her husband, and now you've spoiled it."

"I need to see who won today's stage of the Tour de France," said Fred, fiddling with the remote. "You can watch that silly housewife stuff anytime."

This was too much. First he scorned my nice dinner, forced me to pig out on pork, then he messed up my show's season finale and said I kept the house too cold.

"You've gone nuts ever since that quack doctor said your cholesterol was too high," I snapped, jumping out of my recliner. "Now all you can think about is riding bicycles. You spend more time with those bikes than you do with me!"

Fred got one of those long-suffering looks on his face. "Faye, I've asked you if you want to get a bicycle. I've asked you to take walks with me."

"It's too hot to get out there and walk."

"We can get up early and walk."

"I need my sleep. I don't want to get up early. Why don't you stay home and watch TV with me? You can always take more pills for that cholesterol. You're not a spring chicken. You're supposed to have high cholesterol."

"I don't want to have a heart attack. If you really cared about me, you wouldn't be cooking pork." Then he turned up the volume.

I ran to my bathroom, turned on the fan, and screamed into my fluffy bath sheet. "Damn you, Fred! Damn you!"

I walked back and forth in front of the TV, hoping Fred would comment on my tear-swollen face. He kept dodging around me, waving the remote.

"Hey, I'm trying to watch this," he said.

I stomped into the bedroom and slammed the door. I sat on the bed. Then I got up and slammed the door again. I hoped Fred would get the message. I was hurt.

But it didn't work. I lay down and tossed and turned for hours. How dare he pretend I didn't care about him? Of course I did. I'd eaten pork all my life and it hadn't hurt me. Real men ate meat. They didn't drink pink shakes.

When I woke, the bedside alarm clock said 2 a.m. Fred lay beside me, snoring. Wide awake, I got up and went to the kitchen. I took the dinner I had saved for Fred out of the refrigerator and put it in the microwave. Then I proceeded to eat four more pork chops and all the rest of the mashed potatoes and black-eyed peas. Then I opened a package of chocolate-marshmallow trail mix and ate every last bite.

I sat out on the back porch and watched the sun come up.

My stomach ached and my eyes were sore from crying.

I had had enough.

"What are you doing out here?"

I almost fell off the porch swing. Fred was staring at me from the back door.

"I couldn't find you anywhere," he said. "I was worried."

He was worried? Fred was worried about me? My heart gave a leap.

"I, uh, I must have nodded off."

Then I noticed he was dressed in stretchy black bike shorts and a yellow jersey, one of those silly shirts with three pockets in the back.

"You were worried about me but you took time to put on your bike clothes first?"

He looked at me like I had an extra eye in my head. "What the hell's wrong with you? You know I ride every morning before it gets too hot." He shook his head and went back in the kitchen.

I followed him inside. He was drinking another one of those pink foamy power shakes. He had made a pot of coffee.

I knew I should keep my mouth shut. But I couldn't. "You were worried about me but you stopped to make a pot of coffee *and* a shake *and* put on your bike clothes? What if I'd been kidnapped?"

"Don't be silly, Faye. Why would you be kidnapped? Do I look like Donald Trump? I don't have any ransom money. I'm retired."

He finished his drink, wiped off the pink, foamy mustache with the back of his hand, and tromped across the living room. He was wearing those bicycle cleat shoes.

"You shouldn't wear those in the house!" I shouted.

Fred fastened on his bike helmet and paused at the front door. "Why don't you calm down and drink some coffee? Have you thought about getting back on those anti-depressants?"

Then he slammed the door. I heard those little cleats on his bike shoes going *click click click* on the driveway.

I sank down in my recliner. Anti-depressants, my ass! It was Fred's fault I had that little nervous breakdown a few years ago. He had rail-roaded me into the state hospital with all those lies about my so-called "unstable" behavior. If I was acting crazy, it was his fault.

I tried to be the best wife I could. Cooked my man pork chops and mashed potatoes, kept the house clean, washed his clothes, made his dental appointments. I had even forgiven him for having me locked up. And this was the thanks I got.

* * * *

A few days later Fred said he was going to join a neighborhood bike riding club. "The local peloton," he said, grinning.

The peloton! The word reminded me of penguins. It was a foreign word, of course, everything to do with bicycles was foreign. Whatever happened to those nice Schwinn bikes everybody rode when I was a kid? We didn't have to worry about gears. Now you had to have special clothes, helmets, shoes, and a degree in math just to work those gears. And if you wanted to brake, you had to use the handlebars, not your feet.

The first time Fred persuaded me to get on one of his bikes, I ran right into a mailbox and broke my pinky finger.

"Why didn't you steer away from the box?" he said, picking me up off the ground.

"I couldn't stop. The damn bike wouldn't stop. I kept reversing the pedals and the bike wouldn't stop!"

The neighbor next door paused in his weeding to watch the show.

"How many times have I told you? The brakes are on the handlebars. How hard can it be?"

I was sobbing by this time. I clutched my hurt finger and shouted, "It's not American! It's not American!"

He did take me to the doc in the box and they put a splint on my finger. After that, I refused to go anywhere near those bicycles. A person could get killed.

Anyway, back to the peloton. The neighborhood peloton. All that meant was a bunch of middle-aged men got together and rode down the road, messing up traffic, acting like teenagers instead of driving a car like God intended. And that peloton is a French word. For a gang of guys riding bicycles.

They started meeting on Tuesday nights that summer. Fred didn't get home until after dark. That was okay with me. I could sit and watch anything on TV I wanted and eat as much meat as I felt like without being lectured. Fine, let him go out and fool around. I was glad he was out of my hair.

Then they started meeting on weekends, early in the morning.

"We're riding down to Pecan Grove and back today," he told me one Saturday as the sun was rising. I was bleary and confused. It was way too early to get up.

"Pecan Grove! That's twenty miles away. That's a forty-mile round trip. On bicycles?"

He grinned. "No problem. It'll be great. Next month we're going to ride to San Marcos."

He had lost his mind. He was a retired accountant, not a young stud.

"You're going to kill yourself," I said.

"Nope, I'm in the best shape of my life, Faye." He fastened his helmet and grabbed a sack of bananas and bagels. "You ought to try it. Women who ride bikes have nice tight butts." And with that, he left.

Nice tight butts?

I ran out the front door and flagged him down before he cleared the driveway. He paused, balancing on the bike like some kind of ballerina, and lifted his eyebrows.

"You're in your nightgown, Faye."

"Are there women in your group?"

He stared at me for a moment. "Well, sure, a few."

"Why didn't you tell me?"

He laughed. "Tell you what? Get back inside and get dressed, for God's sake. See you later."

"When later?"

But he was gone, pedaling away, happy as a clam. My next-door neighbor had come out to get the morning paper. He took one look at me and fled back to his house.

I looked down. It was a sheer nightgown and of course I wasn't wearing any underwear. How embarrassing. It was Fred's fault I was becoming the talk of the neighborhood.

All day long I couldn't get it out of my head. *Nice tight butts. Nice tight butts.* Over and over again, like an evil mantra. *Nice tight butts.*

I took off my nightgown and put on a pair of yellow Capri pants and a matching shirt. I looked in the full-length mirror on the bedroom closet door. I turned around and looked over my shoulder. At my butt. My wobbly, untight butt.

I was a retired office worker. I'd spent most of my time sitting behind a desk banging away on a computer. Of course my butt wasn't tight. Now that I was retired, I shouldn't have to worry about my butt. Why couldn't I get fat and happy in my golden years? And why couldn't Fred get fat and happy along with me?

It made me so mad I had to go to the grocery store and fight all the Saturday shoppers. By the time I was through and had almost run over three idiots who didn't seem to notice I was trying to back out of my parking space, I had had it. When I got home I cranked the AC to 68 degrees and opened a gallon of Blue Bell Pistachio Almond ice cream and went to town. I turned on the TV and watched a marathon of *Real Housewives of Atlanta* until I passed out on the couch.

When I woke up it was almost dark. I heard laughing outside on the front porch. I staggered to my feet and went to the door. Where was Fred? He'd been gone for hours.

When I opened the door, there was Fred and a bunch of other people. Well, not a bunch. There were two men and a woman. A girl, really. They were all wearing those tight black shorts. Their bikes were lying right on my front lawn.

Fred said, "I told the guys they could get some ice water for the road."

The two men shook my hand and followed Fred to the kitchen, holding their water bottles. The girl stayed on the porch with me. She must be one of their daughters. She was blonde and blue-eyed with a dark tan and very white teeth.

"Hi, Faye," she said, "I'm Sherri. It's nice to meet you. I asked Fred where he was hiding his wife." She laughed.

I didn't know what was so funny about that. She needed to be careful with all that sun exposure. When she smiled I saw little crinkles around her eyes and mouth. That's what riding bikes did to you. I bet she'd look like a real hag by the time she got to be my age.

"So, Sherri, are you riding with your dad and his friends today?" I was making polite conversation. I don't know why she laughed so hard.

"Oh, Faye. What a sweetheart you are. I retired from the post office last year. I'm the same age as the other guys in the peloton. Maybe a little older!"

She went inside to get some water. I was stunned. That tanned skinny blonde was MY age? No way. No way in hell.

I told myself, don't do it. Don't do it, Faye. But I had to.

I followed her into the kitchen and looked at her butt.

At her nice tight butt.

* * * *

After the little peloton had left with their filled-up water bottles, Fred glared at me.

"What in hell happened to you?"

"What are you talking about?"

"You have green crap all over your shirt. And on your face, for God's sake. What did you do, take a bath in ice cream?"

He pointed at the empty gallon of pistachio ice cream on the kitchen table.

Had I really eaten the whole thing?

I ran and looked at myself in the hall mirror. Oh, my God, Fred was right. I looked like a kid at a birthday party. My face got red. What those people must have thought. Then I got mad again.

"It's your fault," I said, stomping into the bedroom where he was removing his bike shorts. "You didn't tell me you were bringing company over!"

He turned on the shower and stepped in. "Well, hell, I didn't think you'd be covered in ice cream. I was kind of embarrassed."

My rage went through the roof. I jerked back the shower curtain and started screaming at him, while he stood there, helpless, with soap in his eyes.

"I embarrass you! You're the one who rides around in those stupid clothes on your stupid bikes! Most real men watch football on TV!"

He rinsed the soap out of his eyes and turned off the spray. "Why should I watch TV? I'm trying to take care of myself. Maybe you should get off your fat ass and do something instead of eating a whole gallon of ice cream."

"I bet you don't think that skinny blond bitch has a fat ass!"

Fred wrapped a towel around his waist and left the bathroom. "Don't say anything about her," he snarled, as he grabbed for his clothes. "Sherri is not a bitch."

"Oh, what is she now? Your girlfriend? That's it, isn't it? You're screwing around on me with that bicycle bitch!"

Fred finished dressing and pushed me aside—literally, he pushed me—and headed toward the front door, grabbing his wallet and car keys on the way.

"If only I was that lucky, but she's already got a husband. If she gave me the green light, I'd be all over her."

I followed him outside, screaming at the top of my lungs. "You're going to see her, aren't you! AREN'T YOU?" I picked up a rock by the flowerbed and threw it as hard as I could. It smacked him right on the back of his head. He staggered, then whirled around.

Fred looked so mean I was scared. And I'd never been scared of Fred before.

"You crazy bitch! I hope you choke to death on your own pork!"

He got in his car, slammed the door, and peeled out of the driveway like a maniac.

"I hope you die! I hope you die!" I screamed. "You stay away from her!"

The next door neighbor and his wife stared at me from their flower bed.

"Why don't you people get a life?"

I went back in the house, sobbing and screaming until I got sick. I barely made it to the bathroom in time. Ice cream is nasty coming back up.

Looking down at that green puke, I had my light bulb moment.

Fred was going to leave me for Bicycle Barbie. He was in love with her. I kept hearing his words over and over again. About how if she gave him the green light he'd be all over her. But Sherri was married. Maybe she was going to leave her husband. She was nothing but a home-wrecking bitch.

Then I remembered what he said after I hit him with the rock, how he hoped I choked to death on my own pork.

He wanted me dead.

I wasn't crazy. I knew the score. I had watched plenty of those TV shows about husbands killing their wives so they could marry another woman. If Fred watched more TV he'd know that I wasn't as dumb as he thought. I was on to him.

It was him or me.

The next couple of days were hard. Fred treated me like I was some kind of wild animal that ought to be locked up. He slept in the guest room. That is, when he was home. I tried to tone it down, put on a smiley face and act like everything was normal. All the while, deep inside, I was screaming.

I never realized Fred was such a psycho son of a bitch. He acted so ordinary. But I had seen these TV shows where everybody thought the husband was a real nice guy, and then look at what he did. I wasn't fooled. The scales had fallen from my eyes.

The third day after I hit Fred with the rock, I got home from the grocery store and saw the message light blinking on the phone. Fred was out in the garage playing with his bikes, so I pushed the button.

"Mr. Lawson, this is Marty Farr with Downtown Condos. I have a couple of nice prospects I'd like to show you. I bet you'll like them a lot better than the other ones we've looked at."

I erased the message. So, it had come to this. He was looking for a place to live. With that Sherri, no doubt. Probably one of those luxury condos with giant bathtubs and vibrating mattresses and mirrored ceilings.

How could he pay for it? I knew. Over my dead body was how.

I had another thought that almost brought me to my knees. If he wanted a condo, he was going to sell our home. Fred and I had lived here ever since we got married. We had been happy together back then. How did it all go so wrong? How could I live without him?

I looked at myself in the mirror. "Stop that lip trembling, Faye," I said. "You've got to be strong. You weren't raised to be a quitter. You got to fight fire with fire. You got to strike first. It's justifiable homicide. Hell, it's self-defense." I watched those NCIS shows and knew all the legal talk.

I had to be smarter than Fred. For my plan to work, I had to fool him.

He kept flinching whenever he saw me, so it was hard to be patient and pretend that everything was okay. Finally, a few nights after the big blow up, I went to the store and brought home some vanilla-flavored soy milk, chocolate-flavored soy milk, frozen blueberries, and frozen strawberries. I unpacked them on the kitchen table, while he looked on in astonishment.

"Oh, Fred, honey," I said, "I bought these for a peace offering. I know I've been kind of... well, kind of out of control lately. And I want to make up for it. I think it's great that you're making these smoothie things and staying away from pork. I just want to say I'm sorry."

His eyes were like big moons in his face. "Really?' he croaked.

I lowered my eyes and hung my head. "Oh, yes, honey. I don't know what got into me. I called the doctor and I'm going to see about getting back on those anti-depressants." It really galled me to suck up to Fred like this, but I had to get his guard down. After all, I was dealing with a psychopath. It was like playing patty cakes with Hannibal Lecter.

His face kind of melted. "Faye, do you really mean it? I... I can't believe it."

I knew I had him then. He had bitten on the hook and I was ready to reel him in. I wanted to pump my fist in the air and holler "Gotcha!" but I kept my head down and looked sad.

"I want you to be happy, Fred," I said, all soft and sweet.

He was kind of wary, but I just talked to him soft and slow, batting my eyes and acting all lovey-dovey.

He was nervous. He still didn't trust me, but I gritted my teeth and kept on playing along, acting like Betty Homemaker. I even started drinking some of those horrible pink smoothies with him, and asking if he thought I should get a bike. He actually seemed kind of happy about it. Lord, he was such a deceiver! If I didn't know he was screwing around with Sherri and plotting to kill me, I'd almost believe he was sincere.

A few times I almost caved and decided maybe he was a nice guy and maybe I should get a bike, but my inner voice kept telling me to beware. I had to remember all those TV shows about evil husbands and how the trusting wife found out the truth too late. My only hope of survival was to make one of those preemptive strikes.

Since I'd started listening to Fred instead of shutting him out, I learned he and the peloton were going to ride down Route 391 on Saturday and then take the Loop around to the highway. He said they might not get home until after dark, but they'd have their bike lights on. I tucked that information away. You bet I did. A plan had formed in my mind.

All you had to do was look in the newspaper and read how people on bicycles got hit by cars. It happened almost every day. So I figured that come Saturday evening, when it was dusk, and the peloton was out on the Loop, it would be a good time to make that preemptive strike.

I asked Fred to show me where the peloton was going to ride, acting like I was interested in what the hell he was doing, and he seemed pleased.

We drove out in the country, where Fred showed me the bicycle route. The Loop itself, especially the part near the bird sanctuary, was nothing but fields and big trees, no houses, no street lights, hardly any traffic. Yes, it was a good place.

There were a few moments when I had doubts, but I kept giving myself pep talks. I was not going to be Fred's victim. All I had to do was think of that bitch with those sun wrinkles and tight butt taking my place, and I turned as cold as ice. There would be no mercy.

When Fred left to meet with the peloton on Saturday afternoon, he kissed me goodbye. I told him to have a good time. He smiled and said he'd take me shopping for a woman's bike next week. I grinned and kissed him back.

The last kiss.

The Judas kiss.

* * * *

It was dusk when I got in my SUV and backed out of the driveway. People were in their back yards grilling (pork, probably) or inside watching ball games on TV. Even my nosy next-door neighbors were nowhere to be seen.

I watched the odometer like a hawk as I drove through town, hit the access road on the Interstate, and got onto 391. The light was fading. I could see the first fireflies blinking. A rusty old pickup passed me, headed for the highway. Then nothing.

It was almost dark when I turned into the Loop. Tree branches hung down like grasping hands along the narrow, twisting road. Slow down, slow down, I told myself. When I came around a sharp curve, I saw two people riding bicycles just ahead of me on the right shoulder.

I turned off my headlights and slowed down, trying to creep up behind them. I squinted, trying to see in the fading light. A man and a woman were riding side by side. I could only see them from the back, but I knew who they were. The woman had blond hair showing beneath her helmet.

It was Fred and Sherri, together! He had lied about the peloton. It was just the two of them. I bet they were laughing right now, talking about how happy they'd be when Fred killed me and got the insurance money so they could live happily ever after. Well, horsepower trumped bike power. Filled with an inner glow of righteous rage, I rammed my foot all the way down on the accelerator, and aimed straight toward those nice tight butts.

I slammed the SUV right into them.

I almost plunged into the ditch, but managed to fight the vehicle back onto the road. Something was hanging on to my front bumper, dragging on the pavement. In a panic, I hit the accelerator. When I whipped around a sharp corner, whatever it was fell off. I turned my lights back on. I was shaking so hard the SUV was all over the road. I almost rammed into a fence.

When I got back to my neighborhood, I forced myself to drive real slow. I pulled up in the driveway. I got out of the SUV and looked at the front bumper. Oh, my God! It was a mess. There was cloth and metal and the grill was twisted and red yucky stuff was all over the place. Trembling, I opened the garage. Fred kept all his damn bicycles in there so I had to park on the driveway most of the time. I needed to keep anybody from seeing the front of the car, at least until I could get it repaired somewhere out of town.

I ran in there like a crazy woman, grabbing bikes and shoving them across the garage. I dragged them and kicked them, trying to make space for my car. The SUV was still running in the driveway. I had to hide it fast.

Sweating and shaking, I got in the car and started to inch my way into the garage.

WHAM! WHAM!

Something slammed into my driver's side window.

I screamed.

It was Fred! He raised his fist and slammed the glass again.

I rolled down the window.

"What the hell have you done to my bikes?"

Red and blue lights were flashing in my rearview mirror. The neighbors must be wondering why the police were in their nice, quiet neighborhood.

"F-Fred, I thought you were with the peloton," I managed to whisper.

"We finished early," he said, shaking his head slowly, looking at his bikes lying all mangled up on the garage floor. "I stopped by the barbecue place and got some of those baby back ribs you like so much... with potato salad and banana pudding... and stuff."

Car doors slammed behind me. I heard footsteps on the driveway.

My husband was staring at the front bumper of the SUV. He gave me one of those "you-must-be-crazy" looks he was so good at.

The son of a bitch had brought me pork. Just the kind I liked. Full of cholesterol.

I was right all along. He did want me dead.

HAVE A NICE TRIP

KAYE GEORGE

Prissy took great care pulling her salmon soufflé from the oven. It was perfect! Almost perfect, anyway. It had risen beautifully in the center and had only one tiny crack.

"Come and eat, you two," she called into the den. Trey and Abigail, his mother, sat side by side on the couch.

"The poor boy needs to rest," chirped Abigail in that annoying singsong she used when speaking of her darling boy. "You look tired, sweetie. Have you been working too hard in the garden?"

Prissy bit back the answer she wanted to give, but couldn't stifle her laugh. "He hasn't set foot in the garden for two weeks, Mother Abigail."

The tomatoes needed tying up and the squash vines almost hid the weeds. The carrots and lettuce looked good, though. Those were what Prissy had spent Saturday morning on.

"The soufflé is ready." She slid the apple pie into the oven so it would be piping hot when they finished the salmon.

Trey took a couple more crackers with cheese that Prissy had set out, raised his six foot three from the couch, and ambled to the kitchen table.

"Oh, it'll keep for awhile, won't it? I haven't seen Trey for a whole week."

Prissy should have been getting used to this, but—somehow—she always expected Trey's mother to show some consideration. She was always disappointed.

When all three were finally seated at the table with the fallen soufflé and Trey had lit the candles, Prissy told Abigail what they were planning for their belated honeymoon trip.

Her eyes glowed as she told her mother-in-law about the deep, white sand beaches, the snorkeling, the coral reefs of the Virgin Islands. "I think we'll stay on St. Croix, but I want to see the other two islands, too."

"Isn't it terribly hot there?"

"It's tropical. It's about the same year round, nice and warm."

"I don't know why you think you need a honeymoon now." Abigail turned to her son. "You've been married almost a year."

"That's why, Mom," Trey said. "We never had one. Let me show you a picture of one of the beaches. There's an amazing tropical rain forest in the middle of the island."

"We can't wait," Prissy added. "We're looking forward to our get-away so much."

They'd planned to take the trip a few months ago. Prissy had been a nurse for the same doctor for five years, so she had two weeks coming when they got married. After she had gathered a bunch of information on Caribbean islands, plane tickets, and hotel prices, she found out about Trey's job. Trey's boss at the car dealership had let him go for not selling enough cars, Trey said. Prissy later learned he hadn't sold any at all in the year he'd worked there.

Things had changed lately, though. His boss at the hardware store was nicer. Besides, it wasn't hard to sell things there. Prissy was confident he would hold this job a long time. In fact, the longer he lived out of his mother's house, the more grown up he acted. He had finally accrued a few leave days. If they used a weekend, they could spend a week.

"When are you going?" Abigail didn't look pleased about their plans.

Surely she could do without her "darling boy" for a week. Prissy thought Abigail had better get used to it because she intended to take a two-week vacation with the "darling boy" next year.

"Right before the 4th. It's on a Thursday this year, so we'll leave Wednesday night," Trey said, spooning another helping of soufflé onto his plate.

"Be careful," Abigail said. "That's awfully rich."

Prissy noticed she hadn't eaten more than three bites. "Don't you like it? Can I get you something else, Mother Abigail?" The form of address that the woman preferred for Prissy to use—she'd made that clear early on—made her sound like the head of a nunnery. If only she were cloistered!

"No, no, it's fine. I'm not a big fish lover. It can upset my system."

Prissy had never yet fixed anything that agreed with Abigail's peculiar system.

"Have some salad." Prissy passed her the bowl for the second time. Abigail helped herself to two leaves of lettuce.

"Make sure you use sunscreen." Abigail gave her son a worried look. "That sun can burn you quickly in places like that." She turned to Prissy. "He's so fair," she pointed out, in case Prissy hadn't noticed Trey was blond.

"Will you have time to put the plants in for me, dear?" Abigail asked Trey.

"What plants?" Trey asked around his mouthful of salad.

Prissy was going to have to work harder on Trey's table manners. They were all right most of the time, but he reverted when his mother visited. And she was their most frequent mealtime guest.

"When I saw what a nice job you were doing in your flower bed, I decided to put in some annuals."

"What are annuals?" Trey wrinkled his brow.

Prissy clamped her teeth tight. Trey had never touched the flower beds in the front. "I had fun planting the annuals," she said, to set the record straight. "Trey doesn't like to deal with flowers."

"Oh, they're flowers," he said. "Yeah, Prissy does those."

"And?" Prissy prompted.

"You do the vegetables, too, darlin'."

Bless him, that's why she loved Trey. He'd stick up for her when his mother got like that. If he noticed. Being a guy, he was not as quick to see the offensive maneuvers as Prissy was, but his heart was good.

His mother's heart, on the contrary, was rotten to the core. Prissy had decided that, soon after they were married. Lately, thoughts of what life would be like without Mother Abigail had been running through her head, like warm Caribbean breezes running through palm fronds on a beach. And with the same appeal.

Before Abigail left she insisted on conscripting Trey for Sunday afternoon to plant her annuals. That would serve her right, Prissy thought. He'd probably plant them upside down and sideways. Anyway, it was mid-June, too late to put in annuals. They wouldn't thrive, Prissy knew. They would be puny for the rest of the summer after such a late start.

When Abigail summoned Trey to weed her garden the next weekend, Prissy wondered how that would turn out. Trey would probably pull up the flowers and leave the weeds. He'd done that in their own garden last year, which was why Prissy took complete charge.

The next weekend, Abigail said she couldn't come for dinner, but could manage to make it for dessert. Prissy made her best dessert recipe. After all, this was her beloved's mother. Prissy had perfected fudge brownies from scratch, adding a half a pecan atop each piece.

Mother Abigail, who had devoured a bowl of pecans at their house two months ago, said pecans were not agreeing with her lately. She nibbled the edge of one of Prissy's gooey, delectable creations and set it on the edge of her plate, wiping her mouth with the corner of a cloth napkin. Prissy shuddered. That dark red lipstick would be hard to get out of the snowy white linen.

"Trey, darling," Abigail started. Prissy knew it would be a request for him to go to her house, without that bothersome wife, to do another project for her. Sure enough, it was. "Do you think you could come over tomorrow afternoon and help me out with a little project?"

The little project turned out to be putting in a rock garden. Trey returned home Sunday night sore and exhausted.

"You know, she can afford to hire people to do those things," Prissy said, rubbing Icy Hot on his back.

"I know, but she's my mom. She doesn't ask for much."

No, thought Prissy, she only asks for you to spend every weekend with her. Yes, life would be pleasant if the woman were gone. If she were dead. The tantalizing tropical breezes ideas were beginning to take shape, to form pictures in her mind.

Prissy started packing Sunday night, three full days before their departure.

"I think I need the big suitcase, hon," she said, gazing up the pull-down stairs into the attic. "Can you get it down for me?"

"Sure thing."

She stood below and watched his cute butt as he climbed the ladder-like steps. He wrestled the huge suitcase to the opening. The land line phone rang when he was halfway down. Mother Abigail and telemarketers were the only people who used that line, so Prissy ignored it. She stayed where she was, below the steps, ready to catch him if he toppled. But he got it down with minimal grunting.

"Why did you decide to use this one, Priss?"

"Oh, I don't know. The clothes for the Virgin Islands won't take a lot of room, but we might come back with souvenirs."

He hefted the rollie bag onto the bed so Prissy could start filling it. "The phone call was Mom," he said, looking at the bedside phone.

Of course, Prissy thought. She eyed the suitcase, measuring in her mind.

He called his mother back while Prissy started layering underwear and nightclothes into the suitcase.

"You did?" he said. "When? Will you be all right? We'll be right over. No, Prissy will come, too. You should have her look at it."

When he hung up, she stuck her hands on her hips. "What has she done now?"

"What do you mean by that?"

"Nothing, hon. Just tell me what's wrong."

"She slipped on the rocks in the rock garden I just put in."

"It rained last night. Why was she climbing on wet rocks?"

"I don't know. Are you coming with me or not? She thinks she broke her ankle."

When they got there, Prissy felt Abigail's ankle. It wasn't hot or swollen. Prissy wondered if she had fallen at all. "It might be sprained," she said, though she doubted even that.

"How can you tell?" Abigail asked. "It feels like it's broken."

"I'm sure it hurts." Prissy went to Abigail's freezer to see if she had a cold pack. Trey followed her into the kitchen.

"What do you think?" he said.

"I don't think anything's wrong with her ankle at all. It feels fine."

"I'd better go to the hospital and get x-rays," Abigail said as they came back to the den. The woman sat in the recliner with her leg cradled in a pillow on the raised footrest.

"If you'd like, but I can feel that the bones aren't broken." Prissy had gotten a package of frozen peas from the freezer and wrapped them in a clean dish towel. "You may have a hairline fracture, but I don't think it's worth an emergency room visit on a Sunday night."

She held out the improvised cold pack to Abigail, who looked at it as if it were a dead rat. Prissy positioned it on Abigail's ankle herself. "Leave this on twenty minutes or so."

"Would you mind setting the timer in the kitchen?" Abigail said.

"Do you have a portable timer? You should stay off your foot as much as possible until you see if you have a stress fracture. Even if it's just sprained, you should keep it elevated and put ice on it off and on the rest of the day." If Abigail wanted to pretend she had injured her ankle, Prissy could play along.

"I don't need a portable timer. You can turn it off. Or, if you have to go, Trey can do it."

"Mom, Prissy and I need to start getting ready for our trip. I'll be back later tonight to check on you."

"Your trip? I don't understand. You'll have to stay home now that I'm injured. I'll need your help."

"Let's see what your doctor says tomorrow." Trey's voice sounded strained.

"I need to go to the emergency room now, Trey."

Trey gazed at his mother with an unreadable look for several seconds. Then he picked up her phone and dialed 911.

"What are you doing?" Abigail shrieked.

"I'm calling you an ambulance."

"Put that phone down this instant. You'll take me to the emergency room. I'm not having an ambulance."

"Suit yourself." Trey's jaw was tight. "Prissy says your ankle is fine."

"Oh pooh, what does she know? She's not a doctor. She's just making it up. Nurses don't know anything."

"Mother, do not talk about my wife that way."

Prissy felt a glow inside at Trey's loyal defense of her.

"But she's not a doctor. And she doesn't like me. I've always known that."

The glow faded as Prissy gritted her teeth to keep from saying something to the hateful woman.

"Do you want to go to the emergency room?"

"Yes. Please help me to your car."

"I'll call an ambulance. I'm not taking you. I don't have time."

"You don't have time for your poor, injured mother?"

"I'll take you to your doctor tomorrow." Trey spun and walked out of the house.

Prissy, stunned, followed him. In the car, she was silent for a few seconds as Trey started the engine. "You know, if she did hurt herself, someone should stay with her."

Trey turned the car around. "She's faking. She's trying to ruin our vacation."

"I think you're right, but…"

"I grew up with her, you know." He stopped the car three doors down from his mother's house. "Come on, we'll do some diagnostic testing."

Prissy followed him as he crept up to the den window on the side of the house. He pulled out his cell phone and dialed his mother's land line. They both watched as she jumped up and hurried to the phone.

"Mother," he said when she answered, "how did you get to the phone on the second ring?" He held the phone so Prissy could hear the answer.

"I'm hobbling along," Abigail whined. "I'm using an umbrella for a crutch."

The woman was doing no such thing. She had trotted to the phone on two healthy legs and was standing on both of them without aid.

"I'll talk to you tomorrow." Trey cut the connection and they returned home to resume packing.

Monday morning, Abigail's ankle was miraculously better and she called off the visit to her doctor.

On Monday night, Trey started pulling underwear from his drawer so he could pack it. Prissy had spread out her three bathing suits, trying to decide which two to take. Trey stopped what he was doing and looked over at her suitcase.

"Priss, can you possibly use a smaller suitcase?" he asked.

"Well, sure, but… how much are you taking?"

"I thought I'd, well, take the beach towels in my suitcase."

"You don't have to take towels. They have them there."

"Look, I need that suitcase."

"Fine." She knew he couldn't possibly need it. So close to their departure, though, she wasn't going to start an argument. She couldn't help but take her clothes out more forcefully than necessary. Why on earth did Trey think a guy would ever need that much room? That suitcase was big enough to hold a person. In fact, that thought had been possessing her.

Prissy stopped what she was doing and allowed herself to envision Abigail stuffed inside the rollie bag. She smiled as she pictured herself buying a ticket to Madagascar, checking the bag, and waving bye-bye to Mother Abigail. Maybe that would happen some other time.

After she emptied it, she slid the suitcase across the bed to Trey. He put a few socks and t-shirts in it.

The idea of putting Mother Abigail into the suitcase stayed with her at work the next day. She would have to talk Trey out of using that suitcase. She'd talk to him as soon as she got home.

She had to work late because a family brought five children in, all with strep throat. When she insisted on examining the parents, the mother had it, too. It had been an exhausting day. When she pulled her Smart Car into the driveway, she found Trey sitting in his Toyota.

"I have to run an errand," he said, starting the engine.

"Have you heard from your mother?" Prissy asked. It was about time for her to try another trick to ruin their good time.

"She's fine. She said to have a nice trip."

That would be the day. Prissy watched him drive up the block and around the corner. Something was up. He acted nervous and his mother would never, ever tell them to have a nice trip. She had never distrusted Trey, but now she was uneasy. This didn't make sense. What should she do? She followed him.

Tailing a car wasn't all that hard. She knew a bit about it from watching cop shows and reading mysteries. She stayed two or three cars back. He didn't seem to suspect she was there. Soon, however, he turned into the large park at the edge of the city. The park bordered the river on both sides with a bridge across it in the middle of the grounds.

Prissy couldn't follow him into the park. He'd be sure to see her bright yellow Smart Car. She stopped at the entrance, parking at the side of the road, pondering what to do. Trey was acting very strange.

She strolled to the river bank and breathed the fresh, fishy air. She closed her eyes, envisioning lying on the beach, baking in the sun, far away from Abigail. When she opened her eyes, she glanced upriver and saw a Toyota stop on the bridge. It was too far away to tell for sure, but she thought it might be Trey's car.

The driver got out, looked to his left and right, then darted to the back of the car. He wrestled a huge suitcase from the trunk. It looked extremely heavy. He extended the handle and rolled it to the railing. With a struggle, he tipped it up onto the railing and over, into the water.

Her breath caught and her hand flew to her mouth. No, he hadn't! Had he?

She sped home and got herself into the house before Trey got back. She quickly slapped some peanut butter sandwiches together and hacked up an apple. Maybe he'd think that had taken her a lot more time than it had.

He wandered into the kitchen and sat to eat. She didn't ask where he'd gone and he didn't volunteer any information. After they ate, they both went to the bedroom to finish packing for the flight the next day.

The big suitcase was gone. He was stuffing his clothes into the duffel bag. Prissy finished filling the medium-sized one. Should she say anything about the other one being missing? She caught his eye across the bed. He held her glance for two seconds, then looked away.

* * * *

After two awkward, tense days, they settled in and their much delayed honeymoon was relaxing and restful. Prissy wasn't going to mention the big rollie bag unless Trey did. And Trey didn't. Ever.

They returned to their everyday life, tanned and serene. Two weeks went by without anyone asking about Abigail. Prissy thought it was sad that the woman hadn't had any friends who missed her. After another week, Trey reported his mother missing.

The plans Prissy had begun for a two-week getaway were put on hold. They decided they wanted to stay home and relax instead.

Eventually, they sold Abigail's house. The real estate agent said she would play up the appeal of the rock garden, even though the biggest rocks seemed to be missing. After the house sold for a nice amount, the agent said the new owners loved everything, but especially that rock garden.

DEAD MAN ON A SCHOOL BUS

EARL STAGGS

When the phone rang at 6:15 a.m., I groaned, pulled the sheet over my head, and waited for my wife Carol to answer it. Then I remembered she was visiting her sister in Maryland who was going through a rough time with cancer treatment. I groaned again, groped for the phone, and grumbled something that may have sounded like, "Hello."

"Steve," the voice said, "get your lazy butt out of bed and get over here. We found a dead man on one of our buses."

I knew the voice. Lynn Ryan, a good friend. Took me a second to remember she ran the local school bus system. When I didn't respond right away, she said, "Did you hear me? You're still the police chief around here, aren't you?"

"I heard you. Yes, when I went to bed last night, I was still police chief."

"Good. Get over here. We don't know what to do. He was strangled. Wait till you see what he was strangled with."

"What?"

"You'll see when you get here."

"Did you call 911?"

"No, I called you. Should I?"

"No need. They'd just call me. Do you know who the deceased is?"

"One of our drivers. Pete Wilmer."

By then, I was standing and some of the cobwebs had cleared between my ears. "Don't touch anything and keep everybody away from the bus. Don't tell anyone about it until I get there."

"Okay. Hurry."

I stretched and tried to remember if I'd set up the coffeemaker the night before. Carol always did that for me.

After I dressed and made it down to the kitchen, I discovered I had not done the coffeemaker. Fortunately, there was still a cupful in the pot from the day before. I microwaved it and headed out to my car with a hot dose of wake up energy. I promised myself I'd clean up the dishes in the sink before Carol came home.

A dead man on a school bus. That was a new one. I'd seen bodies in cars, on trains, and once even on a plane, but never on a bus. I handled a lot of homicides during my thirty years on the Fort Worth police force, more than I wanted to. That's why I retired from there a year ago and took the job here in Southlake, one of the many suburbs between Fort Worth and Dallas. There hadn't been a homicide here in ten years, they told me.

Once in my car, I called Doc Spradley, the town's beloved family doctor. I told him he was the closest thing we had to a medical examiner. He wasn't happy to be pulled out so early either, but said he'd meet me at the bus lot. Then I called my chief deputy Vic Stack and asked him to meet me there. Vic works the night shift and would finish his tour at eight. If it took longer than that, he'd be happy to earn some overtime.

I'd never actually been to the bus lot, but I'd gone past it many times. It's on Kimball Avenue, on the way to Home Depot. I pulled into the driveway in front of a long, one-story stucco building. Behind the building sat dozens of school buses lined up in rows inside a fenced-in lot covering about two acres.

I spotted Lynn standing on the curb beside the building. Lynn is an attractive woman of fifty-five, the same age as my wife. She's always well-groomed with thick, perfectly shaped, dark brown hair. She and Carol go to the same hair stylist and the same manicurist, shop at the same stores, and attend shows together at Bass Hall in Fort Worth. Lynn's husband Richard and I go to Home Depot together.

"You got here fast," she said as soon as I drove through the gate and rolled the window down. "Good morning."

I climbed out of the car, walked over to her, and kissed her on the cheek. Her skin felt cold and tight. She hugged herself like she might fall down if she didn't.

I placed a hand on each of her shoulders. "Are you all right?"

"Not really," she said. She turned her head to the side. "You might be used to seeing dead bodies, but this is a first for me."

I cupped her chin in my hand and turned her face toward me. "Lynn, I'll tell you a little secret. You never get used to it. All you can do is deal with it the best you can."

She gave me a weak smile and nodded. "I'll try."

"Good girl. Where's the bus?"

"At the end of the second row, number 117. Our mechanic came out to replace a headlight and found Wilmer's body. He called me right away. He and I are the only ones who know about it. I locked the bus to keep it that way. I'll take you to it."

She started walking toward the rows of big yellow buses and I fell in step beside her. Most of the buses were running and lit up. Flashing red and amber lights in the semi-darkness of morning gave the place the look of a lot filled with decorated Christmas trees. Drivers were busy walking around the buses, checking the lights, I guessed.

"One thing hasn't changed," I said. "They look the same as when I was a kid. Like big yellow boxcars. You'd think they'd modernize them and give them a bit of style."

"That's not going to happen. These babies are built for heavy-duty service and safety, not looks. Did you know they're the safest things on the road?"

"No, I didn't know that."

"It's true. You're safer in a school bus than any other vehicle."

"Wasn't very safe for Pete Wilmer."

She sighed. "No, poor guy. By the way, how's everything going with Carol and her sister? Have you talked to her?"

"Every night. Her sister's coming along fine, and Carol said she'd be home in another week."

"And how're you doing on your own?"

"I'm doing just fine."

She snorted. "Sure you are. I know you. You're lost without her. I'll bet you haven't had a decent meal since she left."

"I'm eating okay."

"Yeah, right. Drive thru hamburgers and microwave dinners. And look at your clothes. Your shirt's all wrinkled and has food stains on it."

"I have extra uniform shirts."

"And I'll bet they're all in the laundry basket. You haven't done laundry since she left, have you?"

She was beginning to get on my nerves a little, but I knew she was only doing her job. Carol asked her to keep an eye on me while she was gone. "I said I'm doing fine."

"Liar. Without her, you're a mess. Tell you what. Sunday, you come to our house for a home cooked meal. And bring your dirty clothes. I'll do them up for you. I wouldn't want Carol to come home to a month's worth of laundry."

"Has Richard ever told you what a nag you are?"

"All the time. Be there at three o'clock. No arguments."

She stopped beside one of the buses. "Here we are. Bus 117."

She pulled a key from her pocket, unlocked the door, and pulled it open. Then she took two steps backward and hugged herself again. "I'll... uh... wait here if it's okay. I don't need to see it again."

"That's fine."

I climbed three steps onto the bus and looked down the aisle between rows of seats. Pete Wilmer's body lay on the floor halfway down the aisle. As I moved closer, the first thing I noticed was his bruised and bloody face. He'd been badly beaten. The next thing I saw was something yellow tightly knotted around his neck. I leaned over for a closer look.

I stood up and felt dizzy. I never thought I'd see this again. Once was enough. Two years ago. Cecily Holstrom. Seeing someone strangled with a bright yellow silk scarf once was odd enough. But twice? Hard to believe.

I brushed past Lynn when I stepped off the bus. I'd put Cecily's death behind me, but it came crashing back. I walked to the front of the bus and leaned against the fender. I didn't notice Lynn standing behind me until she spoke.

"Have you ever heard of a man being strangled with a scarf before?"

"Not a man. A woman. A wonderful woman who didn't deserve to die."

"Did you know her?"

"My partner's wife. Her husband John and I worked together for ten years. A cop's partner is family. That made her family, too."

She touched my arm. "I'm sorry, Steve. That must have been terrible. How did her husband take it?"

"Not well. He went to pieces and never came back to work. He totally dropped out. I tried to keep in touch with him, but he didn't return my calls. I went by his house a few times, but he was never home. Six months ago, his phone was disconnected. I tried his house again a month ago, and a neighbor told me he'd gone to Louisiana."

"Did they find out who killed his wife?"

"No."

"How awful."

"Yeah." I straightened up and rubbed my hands together. "But that's history. Doc Spradley should be here any minute, and so will my deputy. They'll take care of the details here. You and I need to talk about the victim."

Doc Spradley and my deputy Vic Stack showed up a few minutes later, and I left them to take care of things. Doc would make arrangements for the victim to be taken to Fort Worth for an autopsy. Vic would go over the bus for anything that might tell us who killed Pete Wilmer.

Lynn and I went to her office. After we'd settled in chairs and had fresh cups of coffee, she asked, "Since it was a woman's scarf, does that mean a woman did it?"

I shook my head. "Not likely. He took a brutal beating from someone powerful, and it takes a lot of strength to strangle someone. When was the last time you saw him?"

"Yesterday morning when he came to work. He did his daily routes and clocked out over the radio at his regular quitting time, about 4:30."

"I'll get an official time of death later, but it looks to me like he's been dead at least twelve hours. That would mean after he clocked out, someone boarded his bus and killed him."

She nodded. "That wouldn't be hard to do. There's a lot of foot traffic on the lot at that time of day, everyone anxious to get home and not paying much attention to who they see."

"Did Wilmer have any enemies here, anyone who might have had a grudge against him?"

"Not that I'm aware of. Kept pretty much to himself and didn't seem to be the kind of man who made friends or enemies. I'd call him a loner. You can talk to the other drivers, but you'll have to wait a couple of hours. They'll be leaving to run their routes in the next few minutes."

"Okay, I'll wait. Someone might have noticed someone who didn't belong here. Have you seen any strangers hanging around lately, anyone or anything out of the ordinary?"

She sipped her coffee and frowned. "I don't think.... Wait! There was someone. For the past three days, a man has been hanging around the parking lot. The first couple of times, he was just sitting in his truck. It was an old gray pickup with a camper top in the bed. We notice strange people hanging around because of the kids."

"Did you happen to get the license plate number?"

"No, I didn't. I probably should have, but I didn't think of it. Sorry."

"That's okay. Did you get a good look at him?"

"Not those first two days, but on the third day, the day before yesterday, when I left at the end of the day, he was standing by the fence. When I got close to him, he turned and walked toward his truck."

"Can you describe him?"

She took another sip of coffee. "Let me see. He was medium height and build, probably in his late forties or early fifties, gray hair. And something else." She raised her hand to her cheek. "There was a scar down the side of his face. It was ragged, kind of like a lightning bolt, three or four inches long."

I felt dizzy again. I couldn't believe what I was hearing. I knew an old gray pickup with a camper top. I'd gone on a number of fishing trips in a truck like that with the man who owned it. And I knew the scar. I was with him when he got it. A guy we were trying to arrest for tearing up a bar went after him with a broken beer bottle.

Why was my partner, John Holstrom, hanging around the bus lot? Was he back in Texas?

I drained my coffee and stood up. "Lynn, when Doc Spradley and Vic finish what they're doing, tell them I'll call them in a little while."

"Where are you going?"

"I have to check something out."

As I walked out of her office, I heard her say, "Don't forget Sunday."

* * * *

Forty minutes later, I turned onto John's street in Colleyville. His pickup sat in the driveway.

I parked at the curb, walked to the door, and rang the bell. He opened the door almost immediately. He smiled.

"Well, well," he said. "It's been a while. C'mon in."

He was thinner than last time I saw him and hadn't shaved for at least three days. He'd always been meticulous about his appearance, but he needed a haircut and wore grungy sweat pants and a faded, wrinkled Dallas Cowboys tee shirt.

He swung the door open wide and I stepped inside. The house had a moldy smell. It needed a good cleaning.

"It's been too long, John," I said. "How've you been?"

"Not too bad."

I followed him through the living room and into the den. He sat at his desk and motioned to a chair beside it. I sat down.

"I figured you'd come," he said. "I didn't think it would be this soon."

"Sometimes things move along quickly."

He smiled again. It was more like a teasing grin. "So you found the guy on the bus."

Why was he so calm and cheerful? He knew why I was there. "Yes, we found him."

He picked up a pen from his desk and twirled it around in his fingers. He did that a lot when we worked together. "Hey, Steve," he said, "want a cup of coffee? How about a beer?"

"Thanks, but I'm good."

"Remember that fishing trip we took to Arkansas? Damn! We put away a lot of beer that weekend, but we caught so many fish, we were giving them away to everyone we knew."

"We had some good times."

"Yeah," he said, his voice barely a whisper. "Great times." He inspected his hands, rubbed them together, and looked them over again.

"I tried to contact you a few times, John. You wouldn't answer my calls, and you were never home."

"I know. I didn't feel like talking to anyone, know what I mean? "

"I suppose so. The guy on the bus, John. Want to tell me about it?"

He carefully laid the pen on his desk. When he spoke, his voice was soft. "Cecily and I were together for twenty-eight years. Twenty-eight wonderful years. We were like two halves of a whole. I couldn't imagine ever not having her in my life. Then, one day, she was dead. It was like every organ in my body had been ripped out. I didn't want to go on without her. I almost didn't. You don't know how many times I wanted to eat my gun so I could be with her."

"I know how tough it was, John. She was special and you two were special together."

He sighed. "Like you and Carol. You have to admit, we were lucky, both of us, to find wives like them."

"I can't argue with that."

He picked up the pen again but didn't twirl it. "I really wanted to end it all, but I couldn't do it. Something stopped me. They came here and took everything that made life worth living. Strangled her with her own scarf. You remember that yellow scarf. Hell, you were with me when I bought it."

"Yellow was her color. She loved that scarf. Wore it almost every day."

John chuckled. "Probably the only thing I ever picked out for her she really liked. Anyway, I couldn't let it go as long as they were out there walking around. You know how I am."

"Yeah, I know. Once you got onto a case, you couldn't let it go until you finished it."

He twirled the pen a few times and tossed it across the desk. "Two men were seen leaving the house that day, but they were never identified. They found one strange print in the house, but when they ran it, it wasn't in the system. Dead end."

"I remember."

"All I could do was hope that someday, they'd find a match. I pestered the hell out of the department and got them to run that print every month for a year. Sooner or later, I knew that guy would get into the system. Finally, he did and they got a match. He was doing a year in Louisiana on DWI charges and driving without a license."

"That's why you went to Louisiana."

"When he was released, I was waiting for him. I knew Colleyville PD would eventually get around to picking him up because of that print, but I got to him first. It took some, uh, unfriendly persuasion, if you know what I mean..." He flashed a grin and a wink to make his point. "...but he gave me the name of the man who was with him that day."

"Pete Wilmer," I said.

"Yes, Pete Wilmer."

"Did he tell you why they did it?"

"Money. They were drinking that day until they ran out of cash. Then they hung around an ATM machine waiting for someone to make a withdrawal. When Cecily took money out, they followed her home. She had two hundred dollars." He looked up at the ceiling for a moment, then squeezed his eyes shut. "They killed her for two hundred stinking dollars, Steve."

"So what happened to the guy in Louisiana?"

John shook his head and flashed the grin again. "Oh, maybe someday if they drain that swamp, they might find him."

"With a yellow silk scarf around his neck? Like Cecily?"

"That's a good possibility."

"And like Pete Wilmer?"

He held the grin and turned toward me. "You catch on quick, Steve. I always said that about you. The guy didn't have an address, but he told me Wilmer worked as a school bus driver somewhere in the Dallas/Fort Worth area."

"And you found him."

"Like you said, I always had to finish what I started. Took a while. I started calling every school district in the area. Finally found him working in Southlake, in your jurisdiction. How ironic was that?"

"John," I said, "you know I have to take you in. You and your truck were seen at the bus lot."

"I know. And you'll find my prints and DNA traces all over that bus." He brightened again. "How about I make it real easy for you? I'll write you a full confession. How does that sound?"

"That sounds fine, John."

He picked up a writing pad from the corner of his desk and stared at it for a moment. "Before you judge me, Steve, let me ask you something. What would you do if someone did to your wife what they did to mine?"

He'd caught me off guard. I couldn't answer.

He shrugged it off and picked up his pen. "You know what? This will take a while. Why don't you get us a cup of coffee? You know where it is." He tossed his head toward the hallway behind us. "There's a fresh pot. Nice and strong the way you like it." He laughed. "Sorry I don't have any doughnuts."

"That's okay. I don't want any doughnuts. Be right back."

I walked into the kitchen feeling something was off. Why was he so calm and jovial? I was going to take him in and charge him with murder. He acted like a man completely at peace with himself, not a care in the world.

His kitchen was a disaster. Plates with dried food on them filled the sink and pots in need of scrubbing cluttered the stove and countertop. The room smelled as bad as it looked. His Cecily had been like my Carol. Everything used in the kitchen had to be cleaned and put away immediately. I reminded myself I had to clean my kitchen before Carol came home.

Then I remembered why I'd come into his kitchen. Coffee. I spotted his coffeemaker beside the stove. It was empty. It wasn't even plugged in.

Dammit!

I turned and raced back to the den. I was halfway there when I heard the shot.

John was slumped over his desk with a pool of blood under his head and a .38 dangling from his right hand.

I should have known. I should have seen it coming.

When I picked up the writing pad, he'd written only one word on it. "Finished."

I fell into the chair beside his desk and looked at the man who'd been like a brother to me for ten years. He was the best cop I'd ever known, the best friend I'd ever had. He finished what he felt he had to do, and he exacted the price for it on himself. If I'd been thinking clearly, I would have seen what he was going to do. Maybe I could have stopped him. Or was it better to let him finish it his way? I don't think I'll ever know the answer to that.

After a few minutes, I called the Colleyville police. While I waited for them, the question John asked me repeated over and over in my mind.

"What would you do if someone did to your wife what they did to mine?"

I don't know the answer to that either. I hope I never have to find out.

HELL ON WHEELS

KATHY WALLER

The day I found Mama stirring ground glass into the filling for a lemon meringue pie, I took the bowl away from her and called a family conference. We had to do something before she dispatched some poor, unsuspecting soul to his heavenly rest and got herself thrown so far back into prison she couldn't see daylight.

The next day, while Mama was down at Essie's *Salon de Beauté*, my brothers and sister and I crowded into a booth at the old Dairy Queen, just across the corner from the library where I worked. The DQ was practically empty. The only customers—besides Frank and Lonnie and Bonita and me—were senior citizens, and most of them had their hearing aids turned off.

When the waitress had delivered our orders and retreated behind the counter to her copy of *People* magazine, I explained why I had called the meeting.

"It hurts me to say it, but the time has come to put Mama out of her misery."

Lonnie stabbed his straw through the plastic lid on his frosted Coke. "Mama don't have no misery. I never seen nobody so contented with her lot."

Bonita poked her pointy elbow into my side and reached across the table to pat Lonnie's hand. "I think Marva Lu's talking about a different kind of misery, baby brother. I'll explain later."

That was a case of the pot calling the kettle black. Bonita's explaining was why it took Lonnie till he was twenty-nine to get his GED.

Frank, sitting across the table from me, grabbed a napkin and wriggled his way out of the booth. "Now look what you made me do. Scared me half to death, making such a mean joke about Mama." He dabbed at his tie with a napkin. "This necktie is a souvenir from when we took the kids to Disney World. That gravy landed right on Donald Duck's tail feathers."

I glanced over my shoulder at the other diners, several of whom were looking our way. "Frank Dewayne Urquhart, stop carrying on and sit back down," I hissed. "You're attracting attention."

Frank unclipped his tie and laid it across the back of the booth. By the time he settled down to finish his steak fingers, the senior citizens had turned back to their burgers.

"Now, quit worrying about that duck's derriere and look me in the eye," I said, in the steely tone of voice I used on seventh-grade boys I found hiding in the how-to books, giggling over *The Joy of Sex*. "I am not joking. This is serious."

Frank stuffed a couple of napkins into his collar and dunked another steak finger. "Serious?" He leaned toward me, his eyes wide and his voice just a whisper. "You want to… put Mama down… just because you saw her add something to the pie? I bet you didn't have your contacts in. Might've been powdered sugar. She's probably practicing something new for the Methodist ladies' fundraiser cook-off."

"The new bishop's going to judge the cook-off." I took a sip of my Diet Dr. Pepper and gave Frank time to think. "I can see the headlines now: 'Murderous Methodist Does in Bishop with Omelet.' And every penny of our inheritance will go to pay a lawyer to try to keep Mama out of prison. Squeaky Vardaman says defense attorneys charge more when the client's guilty. And Squeaky's the district attorney, so he ought to know."

Bonita stabbed me again with her elbow. "Uh-oh, look who's coming." We all followed her gaze.

A bright red Corvette was racing up the street. Ignoring the stop sign, the driver shot through the intersection, just missing a pedestrian, who scrambled onto the high curb and wrapped his arms around a light pole for support.

"There she is, on her way to Essie's to get her hair screwed up." Lonnie grinned. "Man, Mama can drive that car, can't she?"

Frank cleared his throat and wiped his fingers on a napkin. "Yeah, Marva Lu, I see your point."

Bonita wrinkled her nose and wound a blond curl around her finger, a habit she'd gotten into when she was five years old and people told her it was cute. "Why don't we keep a real close watch on Mama and make sure she doesn't have a chance to put anything bad in the food? I mean, killing her seems a little extreme."

"Are you volunteering to babysit around the clock?" I said.

Bonita wrinkled her nose again. "Well, what about putting her in the Silver Seniors Retirement home? We could have her committed. Then she couldn't cook at all."

"No way," said Frank. "Old Dr. Briggs is as loony as Mama. He isn't about to certify her. Hell, there's not a man, woman, or child in the county, including us, who'd dare to cross her. After all, she owns the bank." He wadded his napkin into a ball and dropped it into the empty basket. "You going to convince her to move to the home, Bonita?"

Before Bonita could get her nose back in gear, Lonnie finally caught up with the conversation. He sat up straight. "Killing her? What do you mean, killing her? You saying you want to kill Mama?"

"Shhh. Use your library voice, Lonnie." Bonita patted his hand again. "*Kill* is just a figure of speech. Like one of those smilies we talked about before your test."

I rolled my eyes. "No, it's not a *smilie*. We'd better make sure right now that everybody understands what we're doing."

"I'm not doing anything," whispered Lonnie. "If you're going to kill Mama, I'm heading for the sheriff right now. Move, Frank, and let me out of this booth."

I glared at Frank. He stayed put. I smacked Bonita's hand off Lonnie's and closed my hand around his. Poor Lonnie, he'd always been Mama's favorite, and so softhearted. I should have known our talk would upset him.

I assumed the sympathetic tone I used when citizens called to complain about the library having dirty books. "Lonnie, sweetheart, you heard what I said about Mama's new recipe. And you remember how Uncle Percy died last month, just hours after Mama cooked him a special birthday lunch."

"Dr. Briggs said that was Uncle Percy's ulcer." Lonnie jerked his hand back. "Frank, let me out."

I grabbed his hand again and hung on. "Jasper Alonzo, calm down. I'm going to ask you a question, and I want you to think about it carefully and then give me an honest answer. After that, Frank will let you out, and you can go to the sheriff or anywhere else you want.

"Now, here's the question: How would it make you feel if they put Mama on trial for killing Uncle Percy? Or somebody else she fed bad food to? And what if she had to spend the rest of her natural life locked up in the prison at Huntsville?"

Lonnie's brow wrinkled like it always did when he was turning something over in his mind. One thing about my baby brother, he never made snap decisions. I usually admired him for that. In this case, however, even with the answer so obvious, I threw in some details.

"Think about what prison's like, Lonnie. There wouldn't be a soul Mama knows. And most of those inmates are so common, not our kind of people at all. Mama would have to share a room, and you know how she values her privacy. There'd be no more trips up to Neiman Marcus, and she'd have to dress just like everybody else, in horizontal stripes. She's always been dead-set against horizontal stripes. Essie wouldn't be there to keep up her weekly White Mink rinse, and without that, her gray hair would get that ugly yellow tinge to it. And how would she survive without her Friday bridge club? Think about it, Lonnie. What kind of life would Mama have?"

By the time I got to "yellow tinge," all the fight had gone out of Lonnie. His brow unwrinkled. Tears welled up in his soft brown eyes. It was just the saddest expression I'd ever seen on that sweet face. He looked so miserable I was tempted to toss the rest of my chocolate sundae into the big red waste bin and tell my siblings to forget the whole thing.

But I didn't get to be Director of the Kilburn County Public Library and Archives by caving in to every pathetic face that stared at me across the circulation desk.

"All right, Lonnie," I said. "What's your answer?"

He pulled on his straw but got only a gurgle, so he quit stalling. "Mama wouldn't like prison at all. So I guess I'd feel pretty bad." He shook his cup and managed to suck up one more taste of frosted Coke. "But I still don't feel good about planning to kill her."

I looked out the window. Old Judge Vardaman was shuffling down the sidewalk from the courthouse, heading for the library, where he would spend his usual hour dozing over the *Wall Street Journal.* On his way out, he would tiptoe into my office and sit down for what he called "a little visit with my sweetie-pie."

Bonita saw me watching him and smirked. "Well, here comes Big Sister's gentleman caller. Honestly, Marva Lu, I don't know how you can stand to have that old goat around. He's older than God."

"You should talk," I said. "The way you drool over the old goat's son since he got elected D. A. is a disgrace." I passed the remainder of my sundae across the table to Lonnie and smiled. "Anyway, Bonita, he's not so bad. Goats can be very useful animals." I shouldered my purse and stood up to leave. "Don't worry, Lonnie," I said. "You won't have to do a thing. I'll take care of all the planning myself."

* * * *

When Judge Vardaman sidled into my office carrying his lunch in a brown paper sack, I was ready for him. I reached into the little refrigerator in the corner and took out a strawberry milkshake.

"I brought this over from the DQ just for you," I said. "Let's go up to the third floor where we can be alone."

I led the way toward the stairs. We could have taken the elevator, but the gleam in his eye when I said "alone" told me he'd interpreted the word as permission to make advances. By the time we climbed to the third floor and settled ourselves on the sofa, however, he was so tired I had to help him unwrap his tuna fish sandwich.

The library's third floor had originally housed a small auditorium used for community theater performances. When the dwindling pool of thespians finally disbanded, they abandoned the theater, stage set and all. Most people had forgotten it was there. The sofa the Judge and I sat on was left over from the last performance of *Arsenic and Old Lace*. Handing the Judge his milkshake, I wondered what it would feel like to offer an old gentleman a glass of elderberry wine laced with arsenic.

Then it occurred to me that Mama might already know.

After the Judge caught his breath, he removed a napkin from the paper sack and spread it across his lap. Then he pulled out a boiled egg and tapped the shell on the coffee table. I took the egg from him and peeled it while he opened a small bag of Fritos. I was biding my time, thinking about the best way to bring up the subject I intended to address, when he recovered enough to speak.

"I haven't seen your mama in a coon's age," he said. "How's she getting along?"

He had handed me the perfect opening.

I sighed. "Oh, Judge, I'm worried about her. We all are. Lonnie's so upset he can't even talk about it."

The Judge looked up from his milkshake and frowned. "You mean Sugar's—she's not—"

"Oh, no, nothing like that," I said. "It's… her mind."

"Her mind?" He chuckled. "You know, people who've been around as long as your mama and me—well, our memories aren't what they used to be."

"But it's more than that. I would explain, but it doesn't seem respectful to share intimate details about her condition outside the family—"

"But Sugar is one of my oldest friends. My dearest friends. I don't know whether she ever told you, but I once asked for her hand in marriage."

I knew that. It was one of Mama's favorite dinnertime stories. And it always ended with, "So remember, girls, don't marry the first man who wants to put a diamond on your finger. There's always somebody out there who'll spring for a couple more carats." Then she'd wiggle the fingers of her left hand under the chandelier, so the big marquise cut diamond Daddy gave her sparkled in its light.

I continued my testimony. "Mama imagines things," I said. "Last week, she told Bonita that Harry Truman and General MacArthur came to dinner and stayed overnight, and they kept her awake all night arguing. She had to call President Dwight D. Eisenhower to fly down and make them hush up and leave."

The Judge dismissed my story with the wave of the boiled egg. "A delightful little eccentricity."

"What happen next wasn't at all delightful. She looked out her bedroom window one evening about dusk and saw Mrs. Pancoast taking her sheets off the clothesline. Mama thought the sheets were a ghost fluttering around, so she grabbed her dove hunting shotgun and blasted it right out that second-story window, both barrels."

The Judge's jaw dropped.

"Nearly blew the woman's head off. Bonita and I apologized from here to yonder, but we still had to send Mrs. Pancoast to a fancy spa in New Mexico. She's there till she regains her equanimity, which could take forever. You know that woman's emotions were already jiggly. It's setting us back a pretty penny, too."

I finally had the Judge's attention.

"Ohhhh. That's kind of serious. You tell Frank to take the gun away from her."

"He did. She called Pinkney's Hardware and had another one delivered before Frank could back his car out of the driveway."

The Judge frowned. He picked up a triangle of sandwich with the crust still attached and looked at it, pursing his lips, as if he expected it to contribute to the conversation.

"And this part… I can hardly bring myself to speak it aloud." I took a ragged breath and lowered my eyes. "It's about Uncle Percy." I told him about the ground glass.

The Judge's eyes bugged out. He gasped and choked on a Frito. I whapped him on the back and then handed him a bottle of water I'd brought upstairs for myself.

"Lonnie's staying with Mama now, and they're eating all their meals at restaurants to prevent more culinary disasters. But we can't watch her all the time. We're just out of our minds with worry."

He tsk-tsked and patted my knee. When he finished patting, he let his hand linger. "My poor little honey."

I gently removed his hand from my person and enfolded it in both of my own before filling it with another triangle of sandwich.

"The situation with poor Uncle Percy was dreadful, but there's also the driving. She rampages around in that new red Corvette like she owns the road."

The Judge smiled, and there was a faraway look in his faded blue eyes. "Sugar always loved to drive. She used to tear around in a little baby blue Chevy her daddy gave her for her sixteenth birthday. She'd put the top down, and her blond hair would blow around, and she'd just burn up the road. That little gal was hell on wheels."

I refrained from saying that now she was just plain hell. "Well, Judge, I've heard you burned up a few roads back then, too."

He got a crooked grin on his face, and his eyes twinkled. "Oh, I guess I did my share. Saturday nights, I'd pick Sugar up in my T-Bird, and we'd buzz out to Paradise Bluff, and I'd turn off the engine, and we'd stay there till after midnight, just talking and—" He coughed, and his smile disappeared. "Anyway, we had real good times appreciating the natural environment."

"You still have that old T-Bird, don't you?"

"I do. Still in mint condition. Your mama used to say she'd do just about anything to get her hands on that car. I don't drive it any more, though. Guess I ought to pass it on to my boy before he gets too old to enjoy it."

His boy was Philip Vardaman, Jr., who a couple of years ago had closed his law practice in Dallas, moved back home, and run a successful campaign for district attorney. As a child, he was known as Pip, which, after a time, turned into Pipsqueak, and by the time he got to junior high, everybody in Kilburn was calling him Squeaky. They still called him that.

The Judge swallowed the last bite of sandwich. I watched his free hand, just in case it got any more ideas.

"Maybe that's Mama's problem," I said. "She's too old for that Corvette, but she doesn't know it. What terrifies me, and the others, too, is that she's dangerous. She's liable to have a wreck, run over a pedestrian, kill somebody. Even be brought up on criminal charges. If that occurred, she would be devastated, just devastated."

He shook his head. "Uhm, uhm, uhm."

"Lonnie said the other day—you know Lonnie just idolizes Mama— he said it might be better if Mama did have a wreck—if she could go out doing what she loves best. Then she couldn't hurt someone else, which, if she keeps going like she is now, is bound to happen, and, of course, when it does, she'll never be able to live with herself. Lonnie said.... Oh, no, it's too awful...." I pulled a handkerchief from my pocket and buried my face in it.

"Lonnie said what?"

"Said maybe Mama should have an accident. A bad one... just one car... with no survivors. Said maybe someone could... arrange for her to have an accident, so she won't be a danger to herself anymore." After a few sobs, I raised my head and dabbed at my eyes with the hankie. "The rest of us have begun to think maybe Lonnie's right."

The Judge was quiet for a long time. "That's sounds kind of extreme."

That was what Bonita had said. He and Bonita were two of a kind—no imagination whatsoever.

"Oh, Judge." I looked away. "She's miserable. It's not like the old days, when she was sixteen. She's driving around now like a fiend, probably thinking all the time about how she murdered Uncle Percy, and trying to push that memory out of her mind. It's driving her distracted. Guilt is a terrible burden."

"But, Sweetie Pie, what Lonnie suggested, if you decided to do it, it's a weighty matter. It would require finding somebody to—"

"No, no, no, we wouldn't have to find anyone. We'd do it ourselves. I've already figured out how." I turned my head and stole a look, trying to gauge his reaction to a side of his Sweetie Pie he hadn't seen before.

He gaped. "Well... all right... I guess... But—but—no matter how careful you were, if anyone suspected, the police would investigate, and you could be charged with murder. And prosecuted. And spend the rest of your life in prison."

"I've thought of that. It is a serious consideration. If only we had someone who understood... who would explain things to the right people... and make any investigation go away...." I cut my eyes toward him.

He picked up his milkshake but seemed to forget why, and set it down again. Staring at the cup, he opened his mouth. Nothing came out.

I turned toward him and grabbed his hand. "Oh, if only you would help us. We would be eternally grateful. *I* would be eternally grateful."

He looked at me, his face blanker than I'd ever seen it. I put my hand on his knee and gave it a gentle squeeze. His eyes flew wide open, and he made a sound halfway between a gasp and a giggle.

"Dear Judge Vardaman, could you find it in your heart to help me do this one thing for the first woman you ever loved?"

This time he definitely giggled, and his cheeks turned rosy.

"Oh, I knew I could count on you." I planted a big kiss on his cheek, then jumped back before he could get an arm around me. "We'd better scoot before people begin to talk." I scooped the remains of his lunch into the brown bag and handed it to him. With the DQ cup in one hand, I slipped the other into the crook of his elbow and led him to the elevator.

Downstairs, I walked him to the front door. With his hand on the knob, he glanced around the reading room, leaned close, and whispered, "When is the—departure—going to happen?"

I had that worked out, too. "A week from tomorrow." That was the day before Essie had Mama scheduled for a new permanent. I knew Mama wouldn't want to go out smelling like ammonia.

"Sweetie Pie, do you think it would be appropriate for me to give Sugar a little going-away party, maybe the evening before? Her birthday's coming up, so we could say we're celebrating. I'd like to do something special before she... you know...."

"A lovely idea. You are just the sweetest thing that ever was." I patted his hand. "Now I have to get back to work before the county commissioners find out about our little *tete-a-tete* and ask what we were doing up there."

I winked. He winked back.

I watched from the door. He practically danced down the sidewalk.

* * * *

We spent the next week getting ready for what the Judge had termed the departure.

Of course, worry-wart Frank was all over me about how we would do it. I finally got across to him that it was already worked out: We would give Mama a couple of those pills that knock you out but then let you get up and drive when you're really still asleep—old Dr. Briggs had already given Mama a bottle—and then we'd put her into her Corvette and I would drive her out to Paradise Bluff, which is always deserted these days, the kids having found more comfortable accommodations. Frank would follow in his car. I would park at the edge of the cliff. We would move Mama over behind the wheel, put the car in drive, and let it roll through the wooden barrier and into the gravel pit. Then Frank would take me to my house, and next day Lonnie would wake up and find Mama gone. He would call me, I would call the police, and, with a little guidance, maybe, the police would find Mama. They would think she had been sleep-driving and gone over the edge. In case anyone asked, we'd say Mama had said she wanted to go out to Paradise Bluff for old times' sake, but none of us had had time to drive her.

When I finished describing the process, Frank frowned and said, "We're going to push the car into the gravel pit?"

I said yes, and if he didn't like it, he could do this job by himself. He didn't like it, but all he said was, "Seems like a waste of a good Corvette."

The rest of the family couldn't think about anything but the upcoming party. The Judge got invitations out immediately—very formal they were, too, silver font printed on heavy stock, more like invitations to a wedding than to a farewell party. Bonita said she was going with Squeaky Vardaman and insisted on having a new dress. Mama decided she had to have a new dress, too, but Bonita kicked up a fuss about taking her shopping, and I certainly didn't have time, so Lonnie got the honor. He was happy to do it, since he and Mama enjoyed each other's company.

I didn't buy anything new. The outfit I wore every year to the library volunteer appreciation dinner was good enough: a long black skirt, white blouse, and lightweight black sweater with pearl buttons. This party was the Judge's project. I wasn't going to invest any more money in it than I absolutely had to.

The only hitch in the preparations occurred late Sunday night, a few days before the party. I was in my bedroom, doing some organizing, when the Judge called.

"Sweetie Pie," he said, "this thing you're going to do has my stomach all tied up in knots. I don't think you should go through with it."

I should have known he'd get cold feet.

"But Judge," I said, "you promised. You said you would help, and after that, we would… well…."

"I know, but I feel queasy just thinking about—"

I cut him off. "Well, if that's how you feel, I'm disappointed. But I don't want this to affect your health."

"Oh, Sweetie Pie, I knew you'd understand. Now we can have the party and be happy, and not have to worry about—the other thing. Well, I feel a lot better. I'll see you tomorrow for lunch."

"Before you go," I said, "how's Squeaky getting along with that little problem?"

"What problem?"

"You know, that legal problem he had in Dallas, not long before he moved home."

He was quiet for a long moment. "I don't know what you're talking about."

"Oh, people leave all kinds of documents in library books. Some are so interesting I hang on to them, put them away for safekeeping."

I could hear the Judge breathing.

"It must have cost you a pretty penny to keep Squeaky out of jail. It would be a shame for the story to leak out now." Still he said nothing. "Well, nighty-night."

I eased the phone back onto its base and went back to work. My new aqua Biaggi foldable luggage was open on my bed. I threw in my brand new lacy black negligee and all the bikinis I'd collected over the years I'd been waiting to get out of Kilburn County.

On a whim, I undressed and put one on. I took the pins out of my hair and let it fall past my shoulders, all thick and curly. People called it mousy brown, but if they'd seen it now, they'd have needed a different adjective.

If they could have seen the rest of me, they'd have needed a whole dictionary.

Every night for years, I'd been practicing belly dancing in my living room. There's nothing like belly dancing for keeping your figure.

Standing there, looking at my reflection in the full-length mirror, I approved of what I saw.

I was sure the hunks on the beach at Aruba would approve, too.

* * * *

When I walked into the Holiday Inn ballroom on Thursday night, I felt a momentary regret that I hadn't forked over a few dollars for a new outfit. Everybody who was anybody in Kilburn County, and several people who were nobody at all, were there. Business people, school district employees, county commissioners, the whole sheriff's department, church people, neighbors and friends, everybody who'd ever known Mama was packed into that ballroom. And they were dressed fit to kill.

Frank and Marietta were circulating, making sure the waiters were getting around with trays of drinks and little puff pastries. Frank was in black tie, and for the first time since I'd met her, Marietta had on a dress that hadn't started out as a Simplicity pattern and a bolt of jersey knit. Frank must have loosened up some on her allowance, since he was about to come into money.

Bonita came in, draped in silver lamé and glued to the side of Squeaky Vardaman. A diamond solitaire sparkled on her left hand. Squeaky'd been after her since ninth grade, but she'd said a head cheerleader simply could not date the vice president of the Latin Club without being ostracized from society. I guessed he looked better now he was District Attorney. As for Squeaky, he was strutting around like he'd won the lottery. Bonita's expression, however, suggested she still worried about her popularity rating. Any bleached blonde who turns up dressed in silver lamé isn't easy in her mind.

Mama, on the other hand, had nothing on her mind except having a good time. She and the Judge were holding court, so to speak, in the center of the room, surrounded by admirers. Mama wore a long cream-colored skirt topped with a cream-colored jacket embroidered with gold thread. It was lovely, so tasteful I couldn't believe Lonnie had helped her pick it out. She was giggling like a teenager, and the Judge's face beamed.

Lonnie stood beside the happy couple. He wore a tuxedo, too, and looked so handsome I almost didn't recognize my baby brother. He didn't speak, just stood there gazing at Mama with a loving smile on his face.

I felt another pang. It seemed almost criminal to put an end to such happiness.

By the second course, I could see Judge Vardaman had reached deep into his pocket to pay for this bash. Buying Squeaky out of his little ethical escapade in Dallas had put a hole in that pocket, and I hoped the Judge hadn't overextended himself just for Mama's benefit. She would have been just as pleased with chicken fried steak as with something Julia Child made up. But waiters came around serving one course after another, dishes the Judge had bussed in a French chef from Amarillo to prepare. And wine flowed like water. All those tee-totaling Methodists, and even the Baptists, were downing it like somebody'd told them it was grape juice.

The way they were going, we wouldn't need to take Mama out to Paradise Bluff. We could just stand her in the middle of the parking lot when people were leaving and let somebody run over her.

Needing to keep my wits about me, I did not imbibe. I wanted Frank to follow my example, but whoever had set out the place cards had me wedged between Lonnie on my left and Squeaky on my right. Frank refused to look my way, and he was clear across the big round table, so I couldn't kick him when he started on his second glass. I didn't know what I would do if he got potted and was hung over tomorrow, but he would get an earful from me if he did. And from Marietta, too, if the set of her jaw meant what I thought it did.

Although I didn't partake of alcohol, I discovered that French cuisine can also be a soporific. After all that food, I was downright drowsy. When champagne was poured and the Judge called for speeches, I put on the expression I normally reserved for my nieces' dance recitals, and shifted my brain into neutral. Judging by the number of dignitaries seated at the head table, we could expect a long stretch of tedium.

One guest after another rose to thank to Mama for her contributions to the community: new football helmets for the varsity; Christmas decorations for the courthouse square; carpeting for the Presbyterians; a nursery for the Baptists. The Methodist preacher, a young woman who came to Kilburn straight from seminary, thanked her for replacing the wheezy old Wurlitzer organ with a four-manual Allen loud enough to be heard in Oklahoma. She kindly pretended to forget that at the bishop's getting-to-know-you dinner, Mama hopped up and asked what the Sam Hill he meant by sending us a teeny-bopper in a skirt so short she couldn't even sit on the hem.

It went on and on like that, the microphone passing from hand to hand, people saying what Mama had meant to the town and pretending to mean it. I registered about every tenth word. I was listening instead to the roar of the surf and feeling little waves ripple across bare feet, erasing footprints from warm sands, and a cool breeze moving palm fronds to the strains of a faraway dance band, and inhaling the sweet scent of tropical blossoms floating on salty air, and seeing a moon so big and full you could almost reach out and touch it, and clasped hands holding promise of a closer embrace, and—

I jumped and stifled a scream. Lonnie had grabbed my hand.

"Let go," I hissed. "You're crushing my fingers."

Relaxing his grip a fraction, he leaned close. He had the same look on his face that he had the day he ran into the library to show me a picture of the foal born on the ranch that morning just before daylight.

"This was my idea," he said. He bounced up and down in his chair. "I suggested it to the Judge. Because I knew you felt so terrible."

I nodded. If he wanted to think the party was his idea, that was fine with me.

He loosed my hand and turned his attention back to the Judge, who stood beside Mama's chair, microphone in hand, ready to have the last word.

I glanced at my watch: ten o'clock. I had endured three whole hours of this, and there was more to come. The Judge began to speak. He wasn't known for brevity. As he meandered toward a coherent thought, I stifled a yawn.

"You've all said what a treasure this lovely lady is." He gestured toward Mama, seated on his right. "And to that I say, 'Amen.' She is a woman whose price is above rubies."

O Lord, I thought, don't let him start quoting. That man had everything from the King James Bible to Dr. Seuss stored up in his head. If he got started, we could be here till New Year's Eve.

I picked up my champagne flute and took a swig.

To my relief, the Judge veered back to his own material. "Some of you might know that Sugar was my first girlfriend. My first sweetheart. The first girl I took out to Paradise Bluff. We'd drive up there Saturday nights in the little T-Bird my Daddy bought me—"

O Lord, I thought again. It looked like I was destined to spend the rest of the evening in prayer.

"—and on Sunday afternoons, we'd take her little baby blue Chevy and drive all over Kilburn County, through the back country, sliding on those gravel roads—"

I felt a sudden desire for him to go back to the Bible. That, at least, had an end.

"—and I'll tell you this: Sugar could drive that car. She was a regular Danica Patrick. Sugar was hell on wheels."

The crowd roared. Judge Vardaman paused, looked down at Mama, and rested his hand on her shoulder. She looked up, her face radiant. They locked eyes.

He was a better actor than I'd given him credit for.

"Years ago, I fell in love with Sugar, and I still love her. She should have the best. She should have maids to attend her every need. She should have a chef, so she'll never have to set foot in the kitchen again. She should have a chauffeur, so she can sit back and enjoy the view. And I'm going to see she gets those things."

Across the table, Frank stared into his empty wine glass.

Only Lonnie would meet my eyes, and he was grinning like a possum.

Somehow, I felt, my control over events had slipped. I took another drink of champagne.

When I looked back at the Judge, he was holding out his hand and asking Mama to stand.

"Sugar will have all those things. Because last Monday, her son Lonnie drove us down to the courthouse, where we bought ourselves a marriage license. Tomorrow morning, we're going back to the courthouse and get married." He let go of Mama's hand and picked up his glass. "Please join me in a toast to the soon-to-be Mrs. Bonnie Lu 'Sugar' Vardaman."

The guests joined in a communal gasp. Then they jumped up whooping and hollering and cheering.

"Sounds like our team won the homecoming game, doesn't it?" said Lonnie. "See, Marva Lu? I had a good idea, didn't I? Now Mama won't get into trouble, and the money won't go to a bunch of lawyers."

I couldn't answer. The Judge's words had sucked all the air out of the room. I looked at Squeaky. He was summoning a waiter. His mouth moved but I couldn't hear what came out. I looked past him to Bonita. She was studying her new manicure. Her alabaster skin, reflecting the silver of her dress, had taken on a bluish tinge.

At the front of the room, the Judge was waving.

"Upsy-daisy, sister, dear," said Squeaky. "Your new daddy beckons."

My knees felt like wet sponges. Lonnie and Squeaky each put a hand under one of my arms and hauled me up and started dragging me to the microphone.

"Take your grubby paws off me." They backed away. I smoothed my skirt and lifted my chin and set out on the longest walk of my life. With every step, the future receded before me, the sand and the palms and the sweet scent of bright blossoms—the tide bore them far out to sea, fading in the light of the waning moon.

When even the moon had faded to mist, I found myself standing between Mama and the Judge. He put his arm around my shoulders.

"Ladies and gentlemen." He motioned the crowd back into their seats. "You've had one surprise, and now here's another one. Everybody knows what a fine librarian Sugar's daughter, Miss Marva Lu 'Sweetie Pie' Urquhart, has been for the past twenty years, and we hope she'll be there for another thirty. But here's what you don't know: last week, Lonnie came to me and said he and Sweetie Pie had been talking, and that Sweetie Pie said all she wanted in life was to see their mama properly cared for, and living a happier life than the one she had now."

Applause began. I looked around the table right in front of the dais, the family table, where the Judases gathered. The shadows under Bonita's shifty eyes had turned from blue to indigo. Frank leaned against Marietta and blinked, as if trying to focus. Lonnie and Squeaky were the only ones smiling, Lonnie with the bliss of ignorance, and Squeaky with the smug sneer of the lawyer who would one day inherit everything that should have been mine.

For a moment, I'd forgotten the Judge. He hadn't finished. He gestured for silence.

"Yessir," he said, "this young lady is the one who started the ball rolling. She is as like her mama as two peas in a pod. You know, I always said Sugar was hell on wheels."

He released me to pick up his champagne glass and raised it in my direction.

"Yessir," he said, "Sugar is hell on wheels. But our little Sweetie Pie is hell on wheels with an *automatic transmission*."

* * * *

When the Judge released the guests, the crowd surged forward. Some of them had eyes brimming with tears. They no doubt couldn't wait to tell me what a treasure I was. Others, redneck galoots I went to high school with, probably wanted to make some rude remarks about my automatic transmission.

Before they reached me, I untangled myself from Mama and her new squeeze and ran down the hall to the nearest janitor's closet and hid inside and thought about what to do next.

The only thing to do was get Mama to Paradise Bluff tonight while we were still in the will, before she got married and left everything to Judge Vardaman. If I knew Squeaky, he had a new will all drafted and ready to sign as soon as Mama said, "I do." And Mama was crazy enough to sign it.

Back when all this started, when I determined that a bunch of lawyers weren't going to get my inheritance, I counted the Judge and Squeaky in that number. Now those two would be the first in line.

When the crowd noise had quieted down, I opened the door and peered out. No one was around. I tiptoed back down the hallway to the banquet room, where I found Frank and Lonnie enjoying the last of the champagne.

"Lonnie, what are you doing in here?" I said. "Get out there and keep an eye on Mama." I pushed him toward the door. Then I grabbed the glass out of Frank's hand and slammed it down on the tray so hard I was surprised the stem didn't snap.

"Sober up, Frank," I said.

"Aw, Marvlu, have a heart. Can't shober jus' 'cause you shay to."

I slapped his face. He reeled back against the wall but recovered, eyes focused.

"See how easy it is? Now listen. We have to do it tonight, before she marries that old goat. Lonnie will drive Mama home. I'll follow and give her the sleeping pills and get her to bed. Then I'll send him over to my house to feed my gerbil."

"It takes about five minutes to feed a gerbil. Lonnie'll come back and find us hauling her out."

"No, he won't." Before leaving for the party, I'd let the little rat out of his cage. I knew he'd run and hide under the sofa cushions. Lonnie would be there all night hunting for him.

"Now go out to the parking lot and escort people to their cars. Mama won't leave as long as there's one person to tell her what a wonder she is, and we've got to get her home."

Not chancing another slap, he trotted out of the room.

My presence outside would only prolong things, so I found a clean glass and poured myself some champagne and took a swig. The bubbles tickled my nose. Maybe on the beach in Aruba, I would drink champagne instead of mojitos.

I poured myself a second glass, then uncorked another bottle and moved to a table, where I sat down to wait for Frank to give the all-clear.

Of course, I wouldn't be able to leave town for a while. I would have to get the probate of Mama's estate started, but then I would give it into the care of a trusted attorney, write myself a great big check, pick up my aqua Biaggi suitcase, and jet off to the islands.

I didn't know what the others would do, but I could guess. Bonita would marry Squeaky Vardaman and bore him to death until she got bored and filed for divorce. Frank would buy himself a fancy new car to drive to the bank, where he would stand at his teller's window until Social Security kicked in. He might increase Marietta's allowance so she could buy dresses off the rack. Lonnie would live in Mama's house, keep working on the ranch and adopting stray cats, and be just as happy as ever.

I loved all of them, but right now I wished I could stuff every one of them into that Corvette along with Mama and push the whole bunch into the gravel pit.

I was on my fourth glass of champagne when shouts and running footsteps brought me out of my reverie. The door flew open and there stood Lonnie. His smile had been replaced by a look of mingled horror and despair.

"Marva Lu, I couldn't help it!"

I rose, swaying a bit. "Couldn't help what?"

"It's terrible. She's—You have to come right now." Tears rolled down his face. "Dead. That's what Frank says. Poor Mama."

I followed him through the foyer and out to the parking lot. A crowd had gathered. Three patrol cars, one right after the other, pulled into the lot, sirens wailing. A second later, an ambulance approached from the opposite direction.

Pushing ahead of Lonnie, I shoved my way through the mob. He grasped my arm and tried to pull me back.

"Sister, don't look."

Four men in tuxedos bent over something lying on the pavement.

Frank stood up then and turned around. His face, which had taken on some color when I slapped him, looked ashy in the glow of the street lights.

I grabbed him by the arm and pulled him through the crowd to an open space about thirty feet away.

"What in the Sam Hill is going on here?" I said.

"It's bad, Marva Lu," he said. "Real bad."

I'd already put two and two together. I stepped closer to Frank and lowered my voice. "It can't be that bad. I was sort of hoping she'd get run over in the parking lot. It saves us a lot of trouble."

Lonnie walked over, still crying. I pulled a Kleenex out of my sleeve and handed it to him.

Frank took me by the shoulders and shook me a little. "No, Marva Lu, that's not—Lonnie, it's your fault. You tell her."

Lonnie wiped his eyes. "I wanted to drive her home, but she argued with me, Sister. Said I couldn't boss her around no more, now she had a fiancé. I tried to reason with her, but she set her jaw and got this wild look in her eye, a mean look—"

"Lonnie, get on with it." I was almost ready to slap him, too, when he finally found the main idea.

"She got behind the wheel and started the engine, and the Judge was walking across from where he'd been talking to Squeaky, and all of a sudden, bless her heart, she shouted, 'I'm going to send that man to Paradise,' and she just threw that Corvette into reverse and floor-boarded it, and backed right over the Judge, poor old soul."

"Are you saying Mama ran over him on purpose?" That could throw a monkey wrench into the works. "She must've meant she was going to drive him to Paradise Bluff."

Frank chimed in. "Squeaky sent Mama downtown for questioning. Said he's going to search the Criminal Code, and if he can't find a law she broke, he'll write a new one in the margin."

Before I had time to think, a third man in a tux joined us: Squeaky Vardaman himself, foaming at the mouth.

"I heard Daddy's speech, Marva Lu. Not a half-hour ago, he said you started all this foolishness about old times and fast cars and Paradise Bluff. Well, I'm gonna finish it."

He stopped for a minute to breathe heavy, like the Judge did the day we took the stairs to the third floor of the library. His eyes were so bugged out, I thought he might have apoplexy. I hoped he would. But instead he went on talking.

"That old lady is hell on wheels all right. And I'm going to sue her and get every penny she has, plus oil wells, acreage, and the bank. And then I'm going after you three for letting her anywhere near that car in the first place."

He stalked off to where the men from Sowell's Mortuary were preparing to take the Judge away. Bonita stepped into the spot he'd vacated.

"I'm real sorry, Marva Lu. He gets like that when he's upset." She removed a lace handkerchief from her silver lamé purse and dabbed at her eyes. "I know you're disappointed at how this worked out. If Squeaky gets everything Mama has, I'll make him give y'all an allowance or something."

Frank glanced at his watch and then over his shoulder to where Squeaky stood talking to the deputies. "I've gotta get down to the sheriff's office and try to shut Mama up, goodness knows what she's already told them." He pulled out his wallet and shuffled through a bunch of business cards. "No matter what happens, Mama's going to need the best lawyer we can find."

Somehow, in all the fuss, I'd forgotten about Mama.

"No lawyers, Frank. By noon tomorrow, this will all be taken care of."

Bonita, of course, put in her oar again. "Maybe if Mama tells Squeaky about General MacArthur and Harry Truman arguing in the dining room, he'll just put her in the booby hatch instead of sending her to prison."

"Thank you, Bonita," I said, "for that little ray of sunshine."

"Wait, Frank, I'm going with you." Lonnie kissed me on the cheek, then hurried after Frank, yapping like a puppydog. "Frank, will they make her stay in jail? I'll never forgive myself if they dress her up those horizontal stripes."

Bonita started to follow them. I caught her arm and pulled her back. We watched the deputies take pictures and sweep up shards of broken tail light. In the daytime, the shards would have been red, but the moonless night and the glare of the street lights turned them a dull purple. Everything around us was dull and drab. The only sparkly things were Bonita's engagement ring and her silver lamé dress.

I studied the sparkle.

Bonita tried to pull away. "Let go of my arm," she said. "I've got to get home. These strappy little sandals are cutting into my feet like piano wire."

I relaxed my grip but held on. My mind was going ninety miles an hour. "Squeaky's gone and left you without a ride. I'll take you home." We headed across the lot to my car. I tightened my grip on her arm again, this time to keep her from toppling off her needle heels.

"Oh, dear, Bonita, I just realized I didn't get a chance to tell Squeaky how sorry I am about his daddy. He's probably too upset to see me. Might still be too upset tomorrow." I looked again at her dress, glittering in overhead light. "Maybe you could tell him for me."

Driving along the empty streets, we were quiet, but my mind was still spinning. Then Bonita broke my train of thought.

"I'm sorry your plan didn't work out. I mean, sort of sorry. I know how much it meant to you."

"Oh well." I dredged up a suitable quotation. "'The best-laid schemes o' mice an' men gang aft agley.'"

"Huh?"

"I mean, these things happen. I'm working on another plan right now." We turned down her street. "Do you remember how Squeaky used to love Mama's homemade pies? We could make one right now. An old-fashioned, crunchy pecan pie. Then tomorrow morning you can take it down to the courthouse and cut him a big old slice and tell him how sorry I am."

"That's a good idea. I'd never have thought of it."

I pulled up to the curb. "You go turn on the oven. I'll be right back."

Watching her mince up the sidewalk on those heels, I almost cried. She hadn't even asked where I was going. Mama was right: She always said Bonita didn't have the sense God promised a monkey.

I drove away. At the corner, I floor-boarded it.

If Bonita'd asked, I'd have told her I was on my way to the store to buy fresh eggs and pecans and sugar. I wouldn't have told her I was going to stop by Mama's house to pick up a secret ingredient.

Tomorrow morning, Bonita would take Squeaky a pecan pie laced with ground glass.

Because the Judge was right, too: I was just like Mama.

I was hell on wheels.

RED'S WHITE F-150 BLUES

SCOTT MONTGOMERY

Red Clark was sitting in his recliner, mellowing out with the help of Budweiser and Don Williams, when Billy Ray Bryant called and started the light rain that turned into a shit storm with a chance of fucked-for-life.

"I need a big favor, friend." Leave it to Billy Ray, who took more favors than he gave, to toss in the chaos.

Red had just finished doing all the woman's work Britney asked him to do, and he got Little Dale to take a nap with an hour to spare before Britney got home at her shift from the hospital and he'd have to listen to how her day was. He didn't hold it against her; it just made him feel more and more like a wife since the plant took him down from full time to twenty hours. Only Don William's deep, easy country voice could give him some peace of mind from the world.

"I need you to hide my truck for me. I'm behind a few months and Jerry's after me."

Jerry Coonts was a mechanic who had his own garage, one Red used to work at and planned to buy one time. The incompetent asshole made more cash as a bounty hunter for car dealerships.

"Can I bring it over to your place and hide it in the garage?"

Billy Ray hadn't changed much in the fifteen years Red knew him. They had put together a stock car and entered it on dirt tracks, Billy Ray the driver, Red the mechanic. Billy Ray could always bring the girls and good times. It was when Red felt most free.

As always, good times come to an end. Billy Ray spun out into a crash that was something out of *The Road Warrior*. The bills to fix him took up all the money between them and then some. Another time bad luck killed a bright future.

Red could feel the aggravation hiding the car would lead to. "Bring it over in an hour."

"I don't want to get caught driving it."

"I don't want to argue with my wife, but it'll be a shorter argument if it's in before she gets home."

"You're just cold."

"I'm just married."

"I'll be right over." Billy Ray clicked off.

Red looked out the window at the gray world. It wasn't too different indoors. He thought how the shit never ends.

He had no idea.

* * * *

Red pulled his dad's old Ford out of the garage and Billy Ray pulled his F-150 right in. Red ran in and yanked the garage door down behind him.

Billy Ray jumped out of the truck. "Buddy, you got no idea what you're doing for me, sure do appreciate it."

Red headed toward the string for the ceiling bulb. "I got some." He yanked down on the cord, illuminating the garage and the dust floating around it. The place smelled of grease, paint thinner, and stale ambitions. "How long you need me to keep it here?"

"Two weeks, tops."

In Billy Ray speak that meant three months. Red had no idea why he needed a new pick- up when the economy was in the shit heap.

Billy Ray looked the truck over. "I have some things coming to-gether."

Red knew better than to ask. After he got fired from the plant, Billy Ray went to dealing weed. Got a three-month stay in County a year back. Hard luck drove many of Red's friends to hard time.

Billy Ray looked more nervous than usual. "If I don't come back for it in two, you can call the dealership and get the repo fee."

That didn't sound like Billy Ray.

Red shrugged. "Don't worry."

"Knew I could count on you."

"Sorry this happened."

"Got to take the bad times with the good."

"Don't remember the last good time I saw."

Billy Ray tossed him the keys with a grin. "Sometimes you gotta make 'em."

* * * *

Dinner was about as fun as Red expected it to be. After he drove Billy Ray to his place and came back with Little Dale sound asleep from riding in the Ford, he found Britney in her nursing scrubs, on low burn but getting hotter. She was pissed at work because they put her on a Saturday double shift, pissed to find he left the meatloaf in too long—not that she was a great cook either—and pissed that Little Dale was sleeping now, meaning it would be work to get him to bed later. Mainly she was pissed about the pick-up in the garage.

Red poured gravy over the meatloaf to moisten it some. "It's just for two weeks."

It was hard to tell if the expression on Britney's face was from what he said or what he put on her plate. "You believe that?"

He shrugged. "Said we could turn it in to the dealership if he doesn't pick it up by then."

"Would you really do that?"

Red sat down. "Probably not."

"And you don't think he knows that?" Britney shook her head. "You're too nice."

"There's worse things to be."

"It lets people take advantage of you. You can't even see your own worst enemy."

He bit into his meatloaf. It tasted like a spiced up sponge.

Little Dale ran his fingers through his applesauce, smearing it on his face. They both went for him. Red backed off, let her clean him.

She wiped at their child's fingers. "I don't even know why you like him."

"He's fun."

"He's a drug dealer."

"That we used to buy from."

"We grew up."

"That's just because we had a kid." Red picked up the remote, flipping on the news, hoping the sports would get her attention for a few minutes. Being on the St. Joseph softball team, she was more of the athlete. Was probably why she had so much stamina in their arguments.

"He's going to get you in trouble."

"I'm not knocking over 7-11s with him."

It looked like Britney was going to scrub their son's fingers off. "We're accessories to a crime."

"What crime?"

"Harboring an unpaid vehicle."

"I'd like to see that statute." Red watched a riot in some Middle East country thinking he'd be more comfortable there.

"My friends don't do this to us." Britney scooped up some applesauce with a plastic spoon and tried to get it into Little Dale's mouth. "You're not in high school or on the dirt tracks anymore."

Red turned back around to the TV. They were covering a bank robbery in Ladue. It was nice to watch the rich folks get robbed. However, he lost his smile when the blond male-model reporter said, "Michael Finn, the bank's security guard, died in a shootout outside the bank as the assailants drove away in a Crown Victoria. They were later spotted switching the vehicle with a white Ford F-150. If you have any information, please contact the Ladue police."

They posted the number under Mr. Male Model.

Now Britney was watching.

* * * *

Their argument went for three hours, with a bathroom break and time to put Little Dale down, which took forever, which Britney reminded him was his fault.

She kept bitching at him to call the police. He told her there were a lot of white F-150s; she said it was too much of a coincidence. He said Billy Ray wasn't a killer, she said he was a criminal and was pulling them into a crime.

"He's no good," she told him. "You need to get him out of our lives."

This went on in a loop, over and over, carrying into the bedroom where they fought more than they had sex now.

Britney changed into her least sexy sweat suit. "I swear, your friends can't even be good criminals. Have any of them come through when you had to depend on them?"

No moment came to mind. He pulled off his jeans. "What matters is I'm dependable."

Britney huffed and turned away.

"What's that about?"

She kept her eyes away from him. "Forget about it."

"You were about to tell me I'm not dependable."

"It just feels at times you're more worried about being dependable for guys like Billy Ray than the three of us." She tossed up their comforter and got into bed. "Forget it."

Red just stood there. "We've always gotten through."

"Been harder and harder and we've come close to losing it all. You don't handle all the bills." She pulled the comforter over her and stared up at the ceiling. "You just seem to do for a bunch who don't do back."

Then she looked at him. "What if you made Billy Ray do for us?"

Red didn't ask what she meant. He was afraid he knew the answer. Then she had to state it plain. "Tell him you'll hide the truck for part of the money."

"Then we'd be criminals for sure."

"Not the kind you see put in jail."

"You willing to take that chance?"

"If Billy Ray makes it worth the risk. Think how much we could be out of our hole."

Red did think. He also thought how this would stop the argument, then how it would stop their whole cycle of arguments about money and their life.

"How much should I ask for?"

* * * *

Britney thought twenty thousand was a fair number. Billy Ray didn't.

"This isn't like you at all, pal." Billy Ray was rolling a joint at the kitchen table in his trailer.

"I never thought you'd get me involved in a bank robbery." Actually, Red wasn't too surprised about that.

Billy Ray twisted the end of the blunt. "It just kind of happened. Things were tight, I was really behind payments on the truck, and Tinker needed a wheelman and knew I used to race cars."

"Are you telling me you robbed that bank with Tinker Davis?"

Billy Ray lit up with a nod.

Tinker Davis was the baddest bad guy in Wentzville. He already had done an armed robbery stretch and worked as enforcement for some of the meth crews around. Red once saw Tinker beat Mark Black with a tire iron because Mark made fun of Arnold Schwarzenegger.

Billy Ray took a hit. "I don't know if he'll go for twenty."

Red took a breath of courage. "That's your problem, you got me into this."

"I don't have the money on me."

"Well, get it."

"I'm not bringing this up with Tinker by myself." Billy Ray offered Red a toke.

Red took it. He knew he'd have to be high to do this.

* * * *

Tinker Davis had turned his folks' three bedroom ranch into a shrine to Thirties pulp writer Robert E. Howard. He had the paperback collections from the Seventies with Conan, Kull, and Solomon Kane and the place was practically wallpapered with Frazetta posters, even one from the Conan movie signed by the director and Arnold himself. Little light, the smell of whiskey and sweat, and the hard metal vibrating through the place made it feel like a barbarian's home. No wonder Mark got his ass kicked.

Tinker looked like one of the artist's warriors himself. His long black hair was in a ponytail and he dressed in leather biker pants and vest that showed he spent most of his time in gyms and tattoo parlors. On his chest was a reproduction of a Frazetta cover with Conan standing over a pile of bodies with a sword sticking out of one. A prison job of the stars and bars was on his left shoulder; the right had a bowie knife crossed with a Navy Colt. Below the knuckles of his left hand, the letters L-I-F-E were printed across his fingers, which were wrapped around a Desert Eagle pistol. P-A-I-N was on his right fist knocking Billy Ray down onto the shag carpet.

Tinker put the pistol on Red while he grabbed a broadsword from the wall and swung it close to Billy Ray's throat. "You told him I was your accomplice."

"I had to. Red's cool, though, he's hiding the truck for us."

"I'll hide it for twenty thousand." The gun made Red think about asking that much, but it wasn't worth going through all this for anything less. He wished he'd brought along the shotgun he kept in the bedroom closet.

Tinker's sword poked into Billy Ray's neck a bit. "There some reason I shouldn't kill the both of you right now?"

Red spoke up. "My wife?"

That got Tinker's attention.

"If she doesn't hear from me in twenty minutes, she calls the cops and tells them where the truck is and who used it."

Tinker bared his teeth. "Whole town's going to know before this is done."

"It doesn't have to go further than us for twenty thousand."

Tinker looked at Red with a berserker glare. Red swore his asshole puckered.

The psycho looked him up and down. "Twenty thousand is a lot of money to do nothing."

Since Red didn't have much of a choice, he stood his ground. "I could do something, like drive it to the police station. Billy Ray gave me the keys."

"It would have looked suspicious if I didn't," Billy Ray pleaded.

"Yeah, I see how you did a good job fooling him."

Red felt more relaxed now that that Tinker's focus was all on Billy Ray. "The TV said you guys took over a hundred thousand. That leaves at least forty thousand for each of you."

"I would prefer fifty thousand."

"Split it up any way." Red felt like he had him. "Just better decide soon."

Tinker stood there in contemplation, just like Schwarzenegger in *Conan* before he chopped James Earl Jones' head off.

He put the Desert Eagle down. "Okay."

Red and his asshole relaxed a lot more. He couldn't believe he stared down a gun and got what he wanted. Been a while since he felt this much like a man.

Billy Ray got up. He put his hand over where the sword had cut into him. "So we're all good?"

Tinker's left hand joined his right around the sword hilt. "Still don't have a reason to keep you breathing."

Before Billy Ray could come up with one, Tinker put the blade into his neck. It took two more swings, but he got his head on the floor. Robert E. would have been proud.

Tinker belonged on a Frazetta cover even more now that he was covered in blood. Red noticed some on himself as well. He thought about running out the door, but his legs were jelly.

"You help me bury him without bitching, you can have the twenty thou."

Thank God he'd taken a few hits off Billy Ray's joint. Otherwise he'd really be freaking out.

* * * *

Luckily there was a decent patch of timber behind Tinker's house where they could bury the pieces of Billy Ray after Tinker worked on him with an ax. Apparently, he didn't want to dull his sword. After three hours, they got down to the head.

Red had called Britney a few minutes after they struck the deal and told her they were getting the money, but to call the police if he wasn't home by morning.

Tinker took Billy Ray's head out of the trash bag. "Wish I could mount this on a pike outside the house."

Red looked away. "He was a friend of mine."

"Rather have no friends than pussies like this."

Red shoveled out the last piece of wet earth. "You'd get along with my wife."

"How do you like marriage?"

"It's what got me out here."

"Love." Tinker tossed Billy Ray's head in the hole.

Red covered it with a shovelful of dirt. "You have a girl?"

"Did once." Tinker looked around the woods. "Put her out here somewheres."

"What did she do?"

Tinker shrugged "Something that pissed me off."

Red filled in the last patch. "Can we get to the money now?"

"First we talk to your wife. I want to know who I'm dealing with."

"She's just like me." Red thought burying Billy Ray together would have created some kind of bond. "Just someone who wants some peace of mind for her family."

"I don't really trust your judgment on people." Tinker kicked the ground Billy Ray's head was under.

The cold air went into Red's skin. "I'm not putting my family at risk."

"Then I'll shoot you."

"My wife will call the cops if I'm not home in the morning."

"I'm sure you have your wallet on you with your driver's license. I'll take that off your body, then see your wife. Probably have no choice but to kill her then."

Shit, he was a smart thug.

Red really wished he brought that shotgun now. If he took Tinker home, he'd have a better chance of getting to it and saving Britney. She'd be pissed to see a homicidal maniac with a Conan fixation in her living room, but this was all her idea to begin with.

* * * *

Tinker told Britney she looked familiar. Britney looked down at the Desert Eagle in his hand, then gave Red a look that made him wish he were buried with Billy Ray.

"Tinker just needs some reassurance."

"Your husband complicated matters."

"My matters got complicated when a truck used in a robbery found its way into our garage."

"I told Billy Ray to hide it, I didn't tell him where."

It was odd Britney wouldn't look at him, even though she sounded tough. "You should know Billy Ray Bryant needs supervision."

Tinker stood there and studied her. Red hoped that Britney wouldn't agitate Conan too much before he found a way to get to that shotgun in the bedroom.

Britney raised her hand up. "You want me to take an oath?"

Tinker shook his head. "You got a beer?"

Red went to the fridge. "Got Budweiser."

Britney shook her head. "You boys can't think without alcohol."

Red grabbed two bottles out of the refrigerator. "Mind if I have one?"

"Your house." Tinker told him.

Red grabbed an opener and popped the tops. Red realized "Tulsa Time" was on the stereo. He forgot Britney was a Don Williams fan too.

She huffed. "Can we come to a decision? My shift starts in an hour."

Red handed Tinker his beer. "Britney's a nurse."

Tinker's face lit up. "The nurse. That's how I know you, you're Billy Ray's girl."

Britney looked like she'd been slapped. "What are you talking about?"

"We all hung out two Thursdays ago at The Little Indian."

Red took a step back, taking it all in, as impossible as that was. "Was that when you said you had that double shift?"

"From what Billy Ray told me, she worked a lot of shifts." Tinker looked her over in her scrubs. "Took me a while to recognize you without the denim skirt and your tits hanging out of that red tank top."

"I haven't seen you in that for a while." Red had the dirty look now. "Thought you said that's not how a mother dresses. Course it would look good on a whore."

Britney teared up. "It was a stupid way to blow off some steam. I do love you."

She grabbed his arm. He brushed it off him. Tinker chuckled.

Red felt dizzy. He knew he had to keep it together to survive this, but nobody was helping him. At least he had the beers in his hand.

Tinker grinned at him. "Now I really can't trust your judgment."

Red shrugged. "Well, here's your beer."

He then broke the longneck on the right side of Tinker's head, followed by the other on the left.

He dropped one of the bottles and grabbed Tinker's gun hand.

Britney ran out of the room. Red didn't know if it was to get away or do what he was about to tell her. "Grab the boy and get out!"

Tinker picked Red up by the hair. He could feel his scalp separate from his skull. Tinker charged forward, slamming him into the wall.

Red felt every bone in his body rattle, but he held onto the broken bottle. He slashed the jagged glass across Tinker's forehead. Blood ran down Tinker's face as he let out some kind of war cry. The crazy fucker was enjoying this.

Tinker head butted him in the face. Red heard his nose break, then felt it. He jabbed the broken bottle into Tinker's cheek.

Tinker dropped the gun. Red kneed him in the groin. Tinker let go of Red.

Red dove for the gun. He saw Britney run past with Little Dale. The boy was screaming.

Tinker pulled out a knife.

Red picked up the Desert Eagle and fired. It had a hell of a kick. The bullet obliterated the TV. There went two hundred and fifty bucks.

Tinker went for Britney. Red steadied himself, aimed, and squeezed off another shot. The bullet took off a chunk of Tinker's hip. He fell down past Britney. She got out the door with their boy.

Red got up with the gun. "I think I want half the money now."

Tinker grabbed onto a chair and laughed. He kept laughing as he pulled himself up. Red didn't know what to do.

Tinker got to his feet, covered in his own blood this time, knife in hand, grin on his face. "You would have made one hell of a partner."

He tossed the knife. Red ducked. It gave Tinker enough time to get out of the house.

Red remembered seeing a shotgun rack in the back of Tinker's Dodge and he didn't figure him to be a man who backs down. He ran out with the Desert Eagle. His blood pressure went down a little when he saw Britney's Pontiac race off. It went back up as Tinker pulled the shotgun out of his truck.

Red fired two shots in his direction and missed. "Christ."

Tinker scrambled into the truck. Red made a dash for the garage. He heard Tinker rack load in as he got to the door. He fired off the lock of the garage's side door and got inside and out of the way before Tinker put his own hole in it. He realized that the shotgun would take out the F-150 if he pulled out, then he wished he thought of that a minute earlier.

He had to think fast and did. He jumped up in the F-150 bed and pushed up the spare tire. It was heavier than he thought it would be.

He heard Tinker's work boots stomping into the grass. Red heaved the tire on the floor and jumped out of the bed.

Tinker blocked some of the light he blasted through the side door. His breath grunted through the pain from his blasted hip.

Red rolled the tire.

The tire moved past the door and Tinker burst in. The tire crashed into two oil barrels. Tinker swung the shotgun in the direction of the noise and fired.

Red popped up and unloaded the Desert Eagle. Most of the bullets hit Tinker, putting him down for good. A couple hit the tire. It burst open with green paper. The stolen money exploded across the concrete floor.

Red let out a tired laugh. Now he had to figure out how to hide it all before the police got here. He also had to decide if he was going to tell Britney or not. That conundrum stopped his laughing.

He got the money together in a trash bag, put it under the lining of a can with twigs and raked leaves as he practiced a variation on what actually happened. He heard sirens and walked out to the front yard to greet the police. Looking at the cold, slate gray sky he was reminded that it wasn't too different inside his house.

He shook his head. "Shit never ends."

BIOGRAPHIES

Gale Albright did technical writing at the Petroleum Extension Service of the University of Texas and published several articles in local Austin magazines (*Third Coast* and *Tech-Connect*). Several of her short stories were published in *Blackacre* (UT-Austin Law literary journal), *Sorin Oak Review*, and *New Literati* (St. Edward's University). In 2008, her novel *Eve* won first place in the Young Adult category in the Writers League of Texas manuscript contest. Her short story "Taffy and Lomita" won first place in the Brazos Writers contest. She blogs at http://daralbright.wordpress

Valerie Chandler received her B.A. in Literature from Southwestern University in Georgetown, Texas. She has been a paralegal, a teacher, and a rancher. As a seventh generation Texan, she loves Texas history and incorporates it into many of her stories. Valerie grew up in a family involved with the criminal justice system, (parole officer, criminal justice professor, pathologist, photographer, etc.), so thinking about crime is in her blood. Valerie is involved in church, her community chorus, writes music, and is trying to learn every instrument she can lay her hands on. A member of Sisters in Crime and Writer's League of Texas, she is currently working on her first novel, *Gilt Ridden*, which is set in West Texas.

Kaye George, Agatha-nominated mystery writer, writes several series: Imogene Duckworthy, Cressa Carraway (Barking Rain Press), People of the Wind (Untreed Reads), and, as Janet Cantrell, Fat Cat debuting in September (Berkley Prime Crime). Her short stories appear in anthologies and magazines as well as her own collection, *A Patchwork of Stories*. Her reviews run in *Suspense Magazine*. She lives in Knoxville, TN. http://kayegeorge.com/

Scott Montgomery is the crime fiction coordinator at BookPeople, Texas' largest independent bookstore and a main contributor to its MysteryPeople blog. His short fiction has appeared on the online sites The Big Adios and Slagdrop. He is currently working on his debut novel *Dorothy & the Tinman*.

Laura Oles is a photo industry journalist who spent twenty years covering tech and trends before turning to crime fiction. She is the author of *Digital Photography for Busy Women* and has published over 200 articles in retail and consumer magazines. Laura is a member of Sisters in Crime and Austin Mystery Writers. She has just completed her first novel and is at work at her second one. Website: www.lauraoles.com.

Earl Staggs earned a long list of Five Star reviews for his novels *Memory of a Murder* and *Justified Action* and has twice received a Derringer Award for Best Short Story of the Year. He served as Managing Editor of *Futures Mystery Magazine*, as President of the Short Mystery Fiction Society, is a contributing blog member of Murderous Musings and Make Mine Mystery and a frequent speaker at conferences and seminars. Email: earlstaggs@sbcglobal.net Website: http://earlwstaggs.wordpress.com

Kathy Waller's work has appeared in *Mysterical-E*, Texas Mountain Trail Writers' *Chaos West of the Pecos*, Story Circle Network's *True Words Anthology*, the Story Circle Network Journal, and the *Seguin Gazette-Enterprise*. Her story "Personal Experience" placed second in the 2010 Brazos Writers Writing Contest, and her story "Stop Signs" placed first in the North Texas Professional Writers' Fiction Contest. She is working on a mystery novel. She blogs at http://kathywaller1.com

During **Reavis Z. Wortham's** 35-year career in public education, he also wrote a weekly self-syndicated newspaper column, and for state and national magazines. Upon retirement in 2011, he began writing mystery thrillers. *Kirkus Reviews* listed his first novel, *The Rock Hole*, as one of "the top mysteries of 2011, written to the hilt and harrowing in its unpredictability." *Burrows* and *The Right Side of Wrong* have received critical acclaim from *Publishers Weekly* and *The Library Journal*.

www.ingramcontent.com/pod-product-compliance
Lightning Source LLC
Chambersburg PA
CBHW020650180626
46816CB00003B/1208